OAKWING
A Fairy's Tale

OAKWING
A Fairy's Tale

E. J. Clarke

Aladdin
New York   London   Toronto   Sydney   New Delhi

This book is a work of fiction. Any references to historical events, real people, or real places are used fictitiously. Other names, characters, places, and events are products of the author's imagination, and any resemblance to actual events or places or persons, living or dead, is entirely coincidental.

ALADDIN
An imprint of Simon & Schuster Children's Publishing Division
1230 Avenue of the Americas, New York, New York 10020
First Aladdin hardcover edition May 2017
Text copyright © 2017 by E. J. Clarke
Jacket illustration copyright © 2017 by Jori van der Linde
For information about special discounts for bulk purchases, please contact
Simon & Schuster Special Sales at 1-866-506-1949 or business@simonandschuster.com.
The Simon & Schuster Speakers Bureau can bring authors to your live event. For more
information or to book an event, contact the Simon & Schuster Speakers Bureau
at 1-866-248-3049 or visit our website at www.simonspeakers.com.
Jacket designed by Jessica Handelman
Interior designed by Mike Rosamilia
The text of this book was set in Scala OT.
Manufactured in the United States of America 0417 FFG
2 4 6 8 10 9 7 5 3 1
This book has been cataloged with the Library of Congress.
ISBN 978-1-4814-8191-5 (hc)
ISBN 978-1-4814-8192-2 (eBook)

For Miriam
and Rose

OAKWING
A Fairy's Tale

PROLOGUE

They were finally inside the park.

Rowan's mom paused, closed her eyes, and took a big, grateful breath in. She smiled for the first time that day, standing on the edge of that great, green sea in the heart of the city. An hour on the top deck of a big red London bus had brought them here, with Rowan pressing her face up against the window, arms outstretched, pretending to fly through the streets. Rowan's little sister, Willow, had sat curled up in their mother's lap.

Now they swung their hands together as they strolled toward their favorite spot in Kensington Gardens—an ancient tree trunk that had been carved with all manner of fairies, birds, and fantastical creatures, and painted in glorious colors. The Elfin Oak.

"Pick one, Rowan," whispered her mom as they drew close.

Rowan circled the oak slowly, peering in through the black iron railings that protected the tree. Her eyes passed over the little blue mermaid hugging the bark, the wise orange owl standing watch, the green elf with his head poking out of a hollow. Finally she pointed at a little blue fairy with tiny shells for wings.

"Perfect," said her mom.

Then, as always, the three of them sat on the bench beneath the little clock tower, and Rowan's mom wove a fabulous tale about the character Rowan had chosen. It wasn't from any book that Rowan knew. The story just seemed to spill out as though it had been hiding inside her mom all along, waiting for the right moment to escape. Rowan craned her head back. There was a saying engraved beneath the clock above their heads. *Time Flies.* And it always did.

"Ice cream!" cried Willow suddenly as she wriggled off the bench.

"But the story isn't finished!" protested Rowan.

"Then there'll be some left for tomorrow," her mom said, smiling.

Rowan slumped back and folded her arms. Willow was always interrupting the story at the best part.

"Shall we get a boat?" said her mom. Rowan unpeeled herself from the bench. She was secretly quite excited about the boats, but she wasn't going to show it.

"Bobbily boats!" cried Willow, doing an eager jumping up and down sort of dance.

They bought three strawberry ice creams by the Serpentine Lake, and were about to climb into one of the little wooden rowboats tied up by the shore, when dark clouds gathered in the sky. A breeze started whipping little waves across the water. Rowan's mom closed her eyes and turned her face up to the rain.

"Come, quickly!" she said, her eyes snapping open again as she tugged them away from the lake.

"Bobbily boats?" wailed Willow as she looked behind her.

They were looking around for somewhere to shelter from the rain, when Rowan noticed a huge tree nestled on a sloping bank. It had a great branch curving over right at the top that seemed to hold the rest of it up. It was almost like the tree was upside down. The branches and leaves all cascaded down from the top, creating enormous sheets of foliage that made it look like a giant teepee.

"Tree crying!" said Willow.

"You're right, little one," said their mom. "It's a weeping beech."

The rain was falling in big droplets now, splattering the dusty ground. Rowan's mom pulled back one of the branches like a curtain and ushered the girls inside. They sat, safe and dry, with their backs against the tree trunk as the summer shower fell all around them.

Now Rowan could concentrate on her ice cream. Carefully licking all around it, she pounced on any stray drops that slid down the cone. Willow slowly licked one side of her ice cream, creating a dangerous overhang that was beginning to make Rowan nervous.

"Breathe in, you two. Can you smell it?" Rowan's mom said as she pulled them both close to her.

Willow took a big sniff and got a dollop of pink goo on her nose. Rowan took a deep breath in, but she had no idea what her mom was talking about.

"It's the most beautiful scent in the world. On a

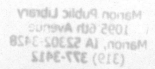

summer's day, when it begins to rain. You catch it only for a moment. But when you do? It's better than the biggest bunch of flowers."

Rowan looked over at her mom. She was gazing beyond the branches, smiling as if she were remembering something. Rowan looked closer. Her mom's eyelashes were dewed with tears. She glanced at Rowan and shook the sadness out of her face.

"The rain's a bit lighter now. We could make a dash for the bus stop," she said, dusting herself off.

"Bobbily boats!" wailed Willow as her scoop of ice cream finally fell off its cone.

"Next time, Willow. Are you coming, Rowan?"

Rowan hung back. The afternoon had been perfect despite the rain, and she couldn't understand why her mom had become upset. She was about to ask, when . . .

"We can come back, Rowan. We can always come back," her mom said quickly. But they never did. That was the last time Rowan saw her mom in the park.

Because the next day was the day that Rowan's mom disappeared.

Chapter One

HAPPY TUESDAY

Rowan always got up before everyone else. She'd sit with a glass of apple juice and gaze out the window, high above the noise of London in their block of apartments, watching the orangey morning light bouncing off the glassy skyscrapers in the distance. She liked to have a little time to herself before the day began, time when she didn't have to worry about the others. Now that Mom wasn't around, looking after the family was up to her.

Dad wasn't much help. He didn't do much of anything anymore. He hadn't done a lot of smiling in the seven years since Mom had vanished. He'd done a lot of sitting. A lot of staring at the TV, even when it wasn't on. He went to his job during the day, though Rowan didn't really understand what it was. Something at the Council that involved computers and talking to as few people as possible. All she knew was that he wasn't really like other dads. Her friends' dads took her friends swimming, or for bike rides in the park, or walked them to school. She would have been happy with any one of those. But Rowan still couldn't swim or ride a bike, because her dad had never taught her. She had to get herself and her sister ready for school every morning. Dad could barely look after himself, let alone his two daughters.

Rowan heard alarm clocks ringing in other parts of the apartment, and the banging and thumping sounds of two people not really wanting to get up. She took a deep breath and headed into the kitchen to start getting the breakfast ready. She opened a cupboard to pull out a box of cereal, but her hand clutched at thin air. "Oh, Dad," she sighed. She closed the door, and noticed the calendar hanging on the wall. Her eyes widened as she saw the date. In one quick movement she grabbed the calendar off the wall and stuffed it beneath a pile of dish towels.

Willow yawned her way into the room, making Rowan jump. Her little sister was wearing pink from head to toe, and had a pair of gauze fairy wings attached to her back with elastic.

"Did you sleep in those?" Rowan asked.

"So. Hungry," Willow said, ignoring the question.

She flopped down into a chair, staring at the space in front of her, as if she were waiting for a bowl of cereal to magically appear. Instead Rowan slid a plate with two pieces of limp, dry toast in front of her.

"Dad forgot to go to the shops on the way back from work," said Rowan.

Willow sighed.

"Happy Tuesday," said Rowan.

Something banged against the hall wall. "Ouch!"

Rowan and Willow looked toward the kitchen door as their dad stumbled in, rubbing his head. He looked like a schoolboy who didn't know how to dress himself. He'd knotted his tie, but it was yanked off center. One side of his collar was up, the other down, and a lock of his hair was stubbornly sticking up at an angle. He had at least shaved, but he'd cut himself a number of times and had little pieces of toilet paper stuck to his face to stop the bleeding. Rowan nodded over at Willow, who immediately put down her toast, wet some paper towel under the tap, and climbed onto a chair. She reached up and plastered her dad's unruly lock of hair down. Meanwhile Rowan straightened his tie and arranged his collar, before rattling a plate of toast onto the table in front of him.

Without a word their dad sat down and began eating. Then he froze with a piece of toast in midair as he stared at the wall. "Something's missing," he said.

"No, no, I don't think so," said Rowan, managing to catch Willow's eye and nodding urgently toward the stack of towels.

"It's the calendar!" Willow piped up. "Rowan put it under the dish towels!"

Rowan rolled her eyes. Willow whipped out the calendar and handed it over to their dad.

"Nooo, Willow," Rowan hissed at her sister. "Put. It. Back!"

Rowan tried to wrestle the calendar away, but she was too late.

"Oh," said Dad as his finger traced across the day's date. The twelfth of August. The day when Mom had disappeared seven years before. The day she'd decided to go to Hyde Park on her own. The day she never came back.

There was an awkward silence around the table. Dad made an odd face. Willow looked back and forth from Dad to Rowan. But neither of them said a word. Dad stared down at his toast.

Rowan broke the silence. "It's time to go, Willow."

Dad's head jerked back up. "I thought school had finished for the summer?"

"It has, Dad. You're taking Willow to Gracie's house on the way to work, remember?"

"Oh. Yes. Of course." Dad rubbed a hand over his face. "Come on, Willow, let's get going."

He wrestled Willow and her wings into a shabby coat she was too big for and bustled her out of the kitchen toward the front door, with Rowan following. He stopped as if he had forgotten something, turning back to look at her. "What about you? What are you going to do?"

"Don't worry, Dad," Rowan replied with a half-hearted smile. She was used to fending for herself. "I'll find something."

"Right. That's . . . good."

The silence grew between them. Then he stepped out into the corridor.

Dad closed the door behind him as Willow's shouts echoed down the stairwell. "See ya, Rowan Snowman!"

"Bye-bye, Willow Pillow!" Rowan called after her.

She turned back into the apartment. Their home suddenly seemed much bigger and quieter. A baby started crying a couple of floors away. Rowan looked at the clock. It was still only nine a.m. She wandered back into the living room and picked up a picture frame from the sideboard. It was a photograph of her mom in happier days, playing a violin in an orchestra. As she looked at the picture, Rowan could almost hear the music. How beautiful it was too. "It's not just a violin," her mom would tell Rowan. "It's a machine for making your heart sing." Once, the apartment had been filled with her mother's music. The violin had been almost the only thing that could stop baby Willow from crying. Though sometimes the hair dryer would do the trick.

Rowan looked more closely at the photo, her finger tracing across her mother's neck, where a necklace seemed to be. It was hard to make out, but the wooden charm looked like a miniature tree. Rowan raised a hand to her own throat, pulling out a necklace from beneath her T-shirt—the charm was a wooden acorn.

A thought suddenly occurred to Rowan. She strode into her dad's bedroom. After climbing on top of a chair, she opened a cupboard above the unmade bed. She pulled out a few old rolls of Christmas wrapping paper, a pile of raggedy towels, and some shoeboxes with high-heeled shoes spilling out. Right at the back of the cupboard was a dusty black instrument case. She lifted it gently down, put it on the bed, and popped the locks to carefully open the lid. Nestled in the case's velvet-lined interior lay her mother's violin. Rowan gently lifted it out, as though she were cradling a newborn baby. She held the polished wooden instrument to her chin, then realized she didn't have a bow. She scrambled back up onto the chair and, standing on tiptoes, saw that in the corner of the cupboard was another case. She stretched as hard as she could to reach for the box, and finally grasped it and pried it open to reveal . . . a long, wooden bow strung with horsehair.

Rowan climbed back down. She held the violin

to her chin and poised the bow above it. She closed her eyes and drew the bow across the violin's strings. *Screeech!* This was not how she remembered it sounding. Rowan winced and tried again. The second time was even worse. Now it screamed even louder, like the foxes that sometimes woke her up at night. It was no use. Her shoulders sagged as she carefully set the violin back in its case and hid everything back in the cupboard. She worried what Dad might say if he knew she'd been in there.

She padded back into the living room and slumped down in the chair that used to be her mom's favorite. It was an old armchair that had seen far better days, and had belonged to Rowan's grandfather. Dad had kept the chair just as it had been when their mom was with them. It didn't face the television like the sofa and her dad's chair, but looked out the window instead. Their block of apartments wasn't the loveliest place in the world, with its cold concrete stairwells and peeling gray paint, but by far the best thing about it was the view. From high up in their tower, they could see all the way across London. Past the London Eye, over the great winding River Thames, through the ocean of brick and glass, and beyond to the little green desert islands of Hampstead Heath and Primrose Hill. Rowan's mom had loved nature. She'd grown up in the country and had never stopped missing it. That was why Rowan and her sister were named after trees. When she couldn't visit the parks, Mom would sit here and gaze at them from afar.

As Rowan sat in her mom's favorite chair, she realized what she needed to do. Today of all days.

Chapter Two

FALLING IN

Rowan went to her wardrobe and picked out her favorite summer dress. It was the only white one that hadn't gone a dirty pink color when her dad had mixed up the laundry by mistake. After locking the door behind her, Rowan pushed the button for the elevator. Nothing happened. As usual, it wasn't working.

She held her breath as she raced down the stairwell instead. She didn't like to think what must have happened on the steps to make them smell like that, because no one ever seemed to clean them. As quick as she could, she was through the double doors and out into the noise and busyness of London. She slipped through the dark, echoing subways beneath the huge roundabout near their tower block, and on the other side jumped onto a big, red double-decker bus parked at a bus stop. Even though she was only eleven, the bus driver didn't give her a second look. She scrambled up the stairs.

There was hardly anyone on the bus, which meant she could sit in her favorite seat—right at the front of the top deck. She stuck her face really close to the glass, held out her arms, and imagined that she was flying through the streets of London, just like she'd done when she used to catch the bus with her mom.

"Hey, No One!" came a voice. A jolt of alarm passed through Rowan. She dropped her arms and turned to see Jade, Jasmine, and Jessica from her class at school. They were sniggering to one another over a take-out box of chicken wings and fries.

"I think her name's Rowan," said Jasmine.

"That's what I said!" Jade shrieked, and they all collapsed into a fit of giggles. If Rowan had made a list of the top twenty people she would least like to see her pretending to fly on the top deck of a bus, Jade, Jasmine, and Jessica would probably have come out as the top three. Rowan turned back, sunk down low into her seat, and wished the scratchy upholstery would swallow her up. A few fries hit the window in front of her, and smeared ketchup trails like tomatoey slugs as they slid down the glass. More loud snorting from the back of the bus. Rowan screwed her eyes tight shut in the hope that it would make her invisible. Surely the girls would get bored soon?

Rowan's hand went to her necklace. She held the acorn tight and stared straight ahead, refusing to cry. Then, just when she thought she couldn't hold on any longer, the *ting* of the bell signaled the bus slowing down for the next stop. The girls all trooped past her.

Rowan stared straight ahead as an empty, ketchup-smeared carton landed in her lap.

"Wanna come shopping with us, No One?" screeched Jade. "You could buy yourself a new mom!"

Cackling with delight, the girls clattered down the stairs.

Rowan blew out a breath, like she'd been holding it in for the last twenty minutes. She gingerly removed the greasy carton from her lap and stared out the window. One small tear spilled from her eye, but she quickly wiped it away.

Rowan got off the bus just before Marble Arch and turned left into Hyde Park, ignoring the street full of shiny white shops to her right. As she walked over the threshold of the park, she stopped, closed her eyes, and took a deep breath, just like her mom used to. That made her feel much better. It was turning out to be a nice summer's day. Even the men shouting at Speakers' Corner couldn't spoil the feeling of peace. She passed the statue of a boy blowing into a horn, who her mom had told her was called Peter Pan, and headed into Kensington Gardens to find the place she had come to visit.

There, guarded by the shiny black railings, was the Elfin Oak. Rowan pressed her nose up against the metal and smiled. It was like seeing an old friend. She saw the little fairy with the two tiny shells for wings, the one she'd picked out that last day with her mom. If only Willow hadn't interrupted the story. Now Rowan would never know how it ended. She looked over at the bench under the clock tower, where they used to sit, and saw another mother feeding a toddler some ice cream. She felt a lump come to her throat, and she knew she couldn't stay any longer. She walked back through the park to the café by the Serpentine Lake. She bought herself a pink ice cream and went to find the weeping beech.

When she got there, she was disappointed to find that a large iron railing had been erected around the beautiful garden that the tree stood in. She turned back round to face the lake. All she could see were happy tourist families seesawing around in their rowboats. That made her mind up for her. She looked around a little nervously, then climbed quickly over the fence, carefully holding her ice cream above her. She dashed across the open grass, through the drooping branches, and into the leafy, secret tent of the tree.

She slumped down with her back against the trunk and licked her ice cream. It didn't taste as good as she remembered. Perhaps it was just because she was older now. The day had warmed up, and the ice cream was melting fast. She licked it all the way around the sides, but no matter how quickly she ate, the melting ice cream kept dripping through her fingers. *Splat!* A big splash of pink landed on her faded dress. She jumped up to try to stop it spilling further, but that knocked the whole ice cream scoop off the top of the cone, and it fell forlornly into the dirt. The day just wasn't working out like she'd hoped at all. Actually, her whole life wasn't really working out like she'd hoped. She knew it wasn't anyone's fault. She had to look after her dad, and she had to take care of her sister, but since her mother had disappeared, there was no one to look after her. There was no one to turn to when Jade, Jasmine, or Jessica said something horrible to her at school. No one to say that they loved her as they gently closed her bedroom door last thing at night. She knew that plenty of kids had a worse time than her, and she didn't want to complain, but she just wished that . . . well . . . *somebody* cared about her.

She sat back down against the tree trunk, holding her empty cone, and stared out through the canopy of leaves at all the happy people. She felt that lump rising in her throat again, and knew that the tears would come soon. She did her best to stop them, but there was nothing she could do. She curled up against the tree, and one by one, small tears slid down her cheeks. She was too sad to wipe them away. The droplets gathered, trembling on the tip of her chin, and then dripped onto the bark of the tree. She closed her eyes tightly, trying to shut out the happy noises of children splashing in the lake nearby. Tired from all the walking and sobbing, she drifted off to sleep. She didn't see her tears slipping through a crack in the bark, straight into the tree's ancient heart. . . .

A gust of wind made the hairs stand up on Rowan's arms. Shivering, she opened her eyes. It was hard to say how long she'd been asleep, but the sky had clouded over. Her cheeks were stiff and salty where the tears had dried. Everything was much quieter than before. And . . . bigger. *Gigantic*, in fact.

Stiffly she climbed to her feet, craning her neck back to gaze up. The tree towered over her like a cathedral. Leaves waved in the gentle breeze above her like giant sails on a pirate galleon. She tried to move, but her feet were stuck in a lake of pink goo. What on earth was it? Surely not . . . *the ice cream*? She waded through it as best she could and scrambled out the other side. This was all just too odd. But then she noticed the cone she'd dropped earlier. It was so enormous, she could have curled up in it and been mistaken for a scoop of ice cream. That was when she realized. It wasn't everything else that had grown big. She was the one who'd grown small. *Tiny*, in fact.

Rowan felt for her necklace, and was relieved to find it was still there. She tucked the acorn pendant back inside her dress and stumbled out from under the tree. Her breath caught in her throat. The park that had been so familiar only a few hours before now seemed like a vast, endless jungle. Giant trees loomed over her, more dark and ominous now against the dusky rose-colored sky. The grass looked like a tangled field of green wheat.

"Hello!" she shouted. "Can somebody help me? Anybody?"

Her voice was so tinkly and small now that a grown-up would hardly have heard it—even if there had been any around. But there weren't. Rowan was on her own in a very strange world.

Or was she?

Something made a fluttering sound in a bush nearby. A bird? The something was moving, making a sound like a violin. Suddenly it darted out from the bush behind her. She spun round. The shape was moving too quickly to make out. Then it made the violin sound again, this time over her head. Perhaps it was a bat whirling around like they did sometimes when she stayed out too late?

A voice sounded from above her head. "Who are you?"

Rowan jumped back and spun around, searching to see exactly where the voice was coming from.

"You there! I said: Who. Are. You?"

Perched high on the uppermost branch of the weeping beech was a boy. He was probably about the same age as Rowan, and roughly the same height. At least, the same height as she was now. His clothes were rusty-brown and crinkled like a fallen leaf, broken up by chunks of armor made of gnarled bark, with a number of small sticks tucked into a belt around his waist. He stood on a branch, shoulders pulled back, apparently not caring in the slightest that he was so high above the ground.

"I, I . . . ," Rowan stammered, wondering how on earth he'd gotten up there.

"Boring!" shouted the boy as he swung his arms in the air and leapt off the branch in an arcing swan dive. Rowan's eyes widened as he fell headfirst toward the ground. Only, he didn't hit the earth below. With wings flashing open from his back, he swooped back up into another tree and hung nonchalantly by one hand from a leaf. His wings buzzed behind his back to keep him aloft.

The boy wasn't a boy.

He was a fairy.

* Chapter Three *
THE REALM OF THE TREE FAIRIES

"Best keep that shut. You never know what'll fly in," the boy fairy said. "Don't you know anything?"

Rowan realized that her mouth was hanging open. She snapped it shut.

"She's new, Aiken," came a voice. "She *doesn't* know anything."

Rowan wheeled round. A robin was standing behind her. Only, the robin was more or less the same height as her. And it was talking. Rowan could feel the blood draining out of her cheeks.

"Sorry," he said. His voice was unexpectedly gentle—although Rowan had never thought before about how a robin's voice should sound. "This must be a bit of a surprise." He took a step toward her, raising a wing in concern. "You should probably sit down."

Rowan went one better and fainted.

When Rowan came round, the robin was fanning her with his wings. She looked at the robin and the fairy woozily. *Oh, yes.* It was still a robin and a fairy. And she was still tiny.

"I'm sorry. We should have done introductions first," said the robin. "I'm Harold, and this is Aiken. Welcome to Hyde Park. Realm of the Tree Fairies. And you are . . . ?"

Aiken smiled, and Harold cocked his head to one side.

Rowan decided this must have been one of those dreams where you know that you're dreaming. Normally that happened just before you woke up, so there was no reason to panic. Yet. If she was nice and polite to the leaf-covered fairy-boy and the talking bird, the dream would probably be over soon. All the same, she began to edge away from them.

"My name is . . . Rowan. I've had what you might

call a strange day, so maybe you can just show me how to get out, and I'll be heading home?"

Harold exchanged a knowing glance with Aiken.

"It is what it is, I'm afraid, Rowan," said the bird.

Aiken dropped out of the tree and landed with a crackle of leaves in front of her. "What my feathered friend here means is that there *isn't* a way out."

Rowan turned away from them. *They aren't real,* she told herself. She pinched herself hard on the tender skin of her arm, but she still wasn't waking up.

"What we're trying to tell you," explained Harold firmly but patiently, "is that it is very dangerous for a fairy out there, in the human world."

If Rowan wasn't going to wake up, she was going to have to deal with this. She slowly turned back around and began speaking to them the way she sometimes spoke to Willow—big sister to little sister.

"Mr. Robin, Mr. Fairy. You've been very welcoming. Thank you. But you know what? This isn't really happening. I'm not really small, and I'm definitely not a fairy."

"Oh," said Aiken, pointing to her back. "Then I guess those can't be wings."

Rowan twisted her head round. Sure enough, sprouting out between the straps of her summer dress was a pair of glistening wings. They weren't like the papery butterfly wings she had seen on fairies in books. They looked much stronger—like a hummingbird's wings. But instead of feathers they seemed to be covered in waxy, transparent oak leaves, layered one on top of the other.

"Why don't you try them out?" encouraged Aiken.

"Agh!" cried Rowan. She danced around and wriggled her shoulders, trying to shrug off the wings as though they were a bug that had landed on her back.

Harold shot a glance at Aiken.

"I know this is a bit strange right now," said Harold, "but it's the same for everyone who falls in. I mean, when they become a fairy."

"We all go a little crazy at first!" added Aiken.

"But I'm a girl. A big, human, totally not a fairy, girl."

"If you say so," Aiken said, shrugging. "Doesn't look like it from here, though."

Rowan tried to shake her head clear, but now the panic was setting in. She could feel her heartbeat going faster and faster, and with it a slightly sick sensation in the pit of her stomach.

"Look, I really just need to get home now," she told the others. "Please. Tell me how to get home."

"Why would you want to go home?" asked Aiken. "No one wants to go *home.*"

Rowan looked at him sideways. She had no idea what he could mean, but she had no intention of sticking around to find out.

"Thank you. Both of you. But I've got spaghetti to cook for my dad, and leggings to sew up for my sister. So I'm just going to head back to the main road and work it out from there."

Unfortunately, Rowan had no idea where the main road was. She knew the park very well, but from this height it looked completely different. She was never normally here when it was dark. But she had to do something. She scanned the tree line and caught sight of a path in the distance that looked to be the size of a highway. She was about to head toward it, when Harold hopped in front of her.

"Do they care about you?" he asked.

Rowan froze. "What do you mean?"

"Just what I said. Do they care about you?"

Rowan wondered if the robin was some kind of mind reader.

"They . . . ," she began, not really knowing what to say next. "They . . . need me."

"That's not the same thing," said Harold. "If you've ended up here, it's because you cried beneath the weeping beech. Like Aiken here. Like all the other fairies in the Realms."

"In the what?"

"You did cry beneath the tree, didn't you?"

"Yes, but . . ."

"Then, welcome. This is your new home. A place where you will be loved."

"Not like the place you've come from!" added Aiken. He seemed to think he was being helpful, but that only made Rowan angry.

"How dare you say that? What do *you* know about my family?"

Harold patted the air with his wings, trying to calm things down.

"Aiken knows that's why he is here. Because he felt unloved when he cried beneath the weeping beech.

That's how fairies become fairies. That's how *you* have become a fairy."

Despite herself, tears began to fill Rowan's eyes.

"But . . . but I still love *them*," she murmured, as much to herself as to the others.

Aiken put a hand on Rowan's shoulder.

"It's *so* much better here. I promise."

Rowan pulled away from Aiken's touch, trying not to notice the hurt expression on his face.

"No, this isn't going to happen," she said. "I'm not staying. I'm going home. Right now."

"We can't stop you," said Harold. "But I *really* wouldn't recommend that you go out there on your own." He glanced over in the direction Rowan had been walking. Rowan could hear the noise of the traffic from beyond the park. It was time to get back to where she belonged.

Rowan took a last look at Harold and Aiken. "It was nice meeting you," she said stiffly. Then she strode off alone.

The park boundary wouldn't have been far at all if Rowan had been her usual size. But for a tiny non-girl-size fairy, she soon realized it was going to take a lot longer to get there. And the longer she kept walking, the darker it got, as night fell all around her. The quiet of the park wasn't so friendly now, and every little rustle in the bushes was like an electric shock to the back of her neck.

An owl hooted off to her left, and she spun in its direction, only to see a giant figure looming over her in the darkness. She shrank back and tried to protect herself, before she realized that the silhouette wasn't moving. It was a statue of a woman with a bow and arrow pointing straight at her, the bronze glinting in the moonlight. *Well done, Rowan,* she thought. *Now you're scared of a lump of metal.* She tried to make herself smile as she walked on, but the grin quickly faded from her face. In the distance she heard something that sounded like a baby crying. Only, she knew it wasn't a child. That would have been a relief. No, it was the scream of something she knew all too well. Something she wouldn't want to meet when she was normal-size, let alone when she was no bigger than a small bird. It was the sound of a *fox*. She felt the hairs prickle on her arms as she forged ahead, one foot in front of the other. She had to get home; that was all there was to it.

Finally she caught sight of orange streetlights ahead. *This will all be over soon,* she told herself, taking a cautious step out of the park gates and onto the pavement. But the instant she set foot outside the park, a sudden wind whipped up to a howl and nearly knocked her off her feet. She struggled forward, pitching her body against the wind. Then an almighty roar rose in the air as the piercing bright lights of the biggest black London taxi in the world came racing toward her. As it whisked by, it created a whirlwind so strong that it sucked Rowan up and threw her back onto the ground with a huge *thump*, covering her with grit and leaves.

"Oof!" she cried as she fell onto her wings, a jolt of pain shooting through her shoulder blades. She picked herself up, dusted herself off, and nervously started walking away from the park again. But before she knew it, there were the lights and the roar of another car, then *another* coming from the other direction. It was like standing on the runway of an airport with huge airplanes taking off right next to her. On all fours she scrambled over toward a stone and clung on to stop herself from being flung up into the air again. She squeezed her eyes tight shut against a blast of grit. She started to sob quietly to herself, wishing she'd just stayed at home—where it was safe.

Finally everything turned still again. Too still. She slowly opened her eyes. A huge, rust-colored fox stood only meters away. Its beady orange eyes were fixed on her. As the two of them made eye contact, its body went rigid. Before she could move, it bounded toward her, saliva dripping from its jaws, tongue lolling out of the side of its mouth. Rowan braced herself for the snap of teeth. The creature's muzzle was centimeters from her face, the stink of stale fur and rubbish bins filling her nostrils, when all of a sudden the beast jerked sideways and hit the ground. Something had barreled into its side, catching the fox by surprise. That same something was now pecking at its face, and the fox rolled and yelped, struggling to brush the thing off.

"Not that I should care about someone as rude as you," came a voice from behind Rowan, "but if I were in your wings, I'd get back into the park while Harold is distracting that fox."

Rowan scrambled up and raced back to Aiken and

the safety of the park. Behind her she heard a final howl and the fox running off into the night.

"Sometimes I suppose you have to see something to believe it," said a slightly bedraggled-looking Harold when he hopped back through the gates. "As I explained, it's dangerous out there for fairies. In the future it will save us both a lot of time if you just take my word for it."

Aiken pulled Harold aside for a second and whispered into the robin's ear. Not very quietly—Rowan could hear every word.

"Was it one of *his*?" Aiken hissed.

Harold looked at his clawed feet. "Undoubtedly," he said.

Rowan felt a shiver run through her body. She had no idea what they were talking about, but right now there was only one question on her mind. "So there's no going back?"

Harold met her gaze. "It is what it is," he said. This time Rowan didn't try to argue.

Chapter Four

THE PARROT AND QUEEN VICTORIA

"First things first," said Harold as they hopped back through the park. Aiken buzzed round overhead. "The world that you come from—the human world—is very, very dangerous for a fairy. That's why none of us live there."

"None of *us* . . . ?" began Rowan.

"As I was saying," Harold said stiffly. He didn't seem to like being interrupted. "There are cars and cats and foxes and—worst of all—people. Any number of things that could be the end of a fairy."

"But my dad, my sister—they're people. They could help?"

Harold stopped dead.

"You need to understand a few things, and you need to understand them right now." Harold looked about as serious as a robin can look.

"Number one. Maybe you didn't understand when you were nearly run over and eaten, but it's *dangerous* out there. You took one step outside the park, and *that* all happened. How many steps are there between you and this family of yours? How many more opportunities to get blown away, swallowed, or crushed?"

Rowan really didn't like where this conversation was going.

"Number two. Let's just say you survive all those thousands of steps, and you finally make it back to your family. What are you going to do then? If you don't give your dad a heart attack when he sees you, what's he going to do with a daughter who can sit in the palm of his hand? Keep you in a birdcage? Pack you off to the circus?"

Rowan was getting quite upset now.

"He wouldn't do that to me."

"No?" said Harold. "Half an hour ago you thought nobody loved you, and now you think he'll welcome you back with open arms like nothing's changed?"

Rowan's lip began to tremble.

"That's a bit rough on her, old beak face," said Aiken. "Just 'cause she doesn't want to stay doesn't mean—"

"Then I'll have to get back to being me first," Rowan interrupted.

"Number three," said Harold. "Becoming a fairy is a one-way ticket."

Rowan summoned up a little more courage.

"Then I'll have to be the first one to get a return."

"That way only ends in disappointment," replied Harold, hopping off ahead.

Aiken shouted after him, "What about the Heart of Oak?"

Harold's shoulders slumped. "Much better just to get used to things as they are. Save yourself a lot of heartache," he said without looking round.

"Hang on," said Rowan. "What's the Heart of Oak?"

Aiken took a deep breath, clearly glad to finally be of some use. "It is said that '*When the fairy of most power unlocks the Heart of Oak, they shall become human again.*'"

"But why didn't you tell me that before?" asked

Rowan, instantly encouraged. "Where is it and how do we unlock it?"

"Ah," said Aiken. "That's sort of the tricky part. No one actually knows what the Heart of Oak is. Much less how to use it."

"It's just a silly saying," added Harold, turning to Aiken. "And you'd do well not to get her hopes up."

"But what if it were true? What if it exists?" said Rowan.

"Now look what you've done," muttered Harold.

"Is there anyone who could help us find it?" asked Rowan.

"Us?" said Harold.

"Okay, me. Is there anyone who could help me find it?"

"The GodMother!" blurted out Aiken.

"The GodMother has no more idea what the Heart of Oak is than you do," said Harold.

"Please, Harold," begged Rowan. "I know you think this is all a huge waste of your time, and I'm sorry I'm not happier about being a fairy. But if there was even the faintest chance I could get back home, I would take it."

Harold looked long and hard at Rowan. Then his gaze softened. Something had clearly shifted in him.

"The GodMother has always cared for the restless souls of the Realms," he said. "Maybe she can help talk some sense into you. . . ."

"Yes!" shouted Aiken. Rowan allowed herself her first smile in a while.

"Can you fly?" asked Harold. "We wouldn't last five minutes trying to get to the GodMother on foot. But in the sky we'd have a chance."

It hadn't occurred to Rowan that these wings sprouting from her back might actually work.

"Like this!" shouted Aiken as he spiraled and spun above them, showing off.

Harold shot Aiken a stern look, and the boy fairy went off to sulk on a branch. Rowan glanced over her shoulder at the wings behind her, unsure what she was supposed to do to make them work. She shifted her shoulder blades back and sort of rolled them around, and began to feel the muscles that moved the wings. All of a sudden something seemed to click into gear, and her wings buzzed, making the same awful sound that her mother's violin had made when she'd tried to play it that morning. Aiken and Harold winced.

"Sorry," said Rowan, though she wasn't quite sure why she was apologizing.

She tried again. Although the wings still made a horrible grating sound, she began to lift slowly into the air. A smile spread across her face, but then all of a sudden she jerked sideways and slammed into the ground.

Harold hopped over to see if she was all right. "Wings can be pretty tricky to control when they're new." Rowan picked herself up gingerly. "Maybe we should leave that for another day. You can ride on my back until you get used to them." Harold leaned over and stretched out a wing for Rowan to climb up.

Rowan couldn't quite believe what she was doing—she'd never even sat on a bike before, never mind a bird in the park—but she put one foot on Harold's wing and swung the other over his body. He was downy soft to sit on, but still very delicate-feeling and a bit twitchy. She could feel his heart beating beneath her.

"So," said Rowan, "how do we get to this GodMother person?"

"She lives with the Fairies of the Birds in the Park

of St. James," said Harold. "But she's not a person. In fact, I don't know what she'll be."

"That's super-helpful," said Aiken.

"That's as much as I can tell you for now. Climb on," replied Harold.

"Hang on," said Aiken. "You want me to come too?"

"What's wrong?" asked Rowan.

"I've never been outside of Hyde Park before," Aiken said quietly.

"We'll need all the help we can get, given how incredibly dangerous this is going to be," said Harold. He seemed to enjoy making Aiken feel uncomfortable. "Maybe you'd prefer to stay here? Do a few loop-the-loops? Sharpen a few twigs?" He pointed a wing tip at the array of sharp twigs tucked into the belt around Aiken's waist.

Aiken stuck out his chest. Rowan sensed that he didn't want to look bad in front of her.

"No, no. I've more than enough twigs to last me awhile. I'd be very happy to. You know. Come with you."

"And I can't promise you'd ever come back."

Aiken looked even less sure. "Of course. Goes with the territory."

Aiken climbed on behind Rowan and she gave him a little kiss on the cheek.

"Thank you," she said.

Aiken's rusty-colored cheeks went a slightly redder shade of brown.

"So, what should I hold on toooooo . . . !" she shouted as Harold sprang off. Rowan flung her arms around his neck to stop herself from falling off. Before she knew it, the three of them were arcing up in the air.

They whisked through the trees of the park, and Rowan looked around in wonder. This wasn't like being in a plane. This was a different kind of flying altogether—darting from bush to bush, over branches and under leaves. It was more like one of the rides at the fun fair that whirl round really fast and go up and down. Those rides made her feel a bit sick when she went on them, but there was something about being on Harold's back, her body pressed against the warmth of his feathers, that made her feel much calmer.

"Why don't you know what the GodMother will *be*, Harold?" Rowan shouted into his ear.

"Maybe it's time I told you a bit more about the Fairy Realms," replied Harold over his shoulder.

"I get the feeling there's a history lesson coming," groaned Aiken.

They sped through the darkness and lifted up over the street lit illumination of Park Lane, the traffic noise fading beneath them. As they flew, Harold began his story.

"Long ago," he said, "before cities, and cars, and electric lights, fairies were everywhere. They lived happily in trees and hedgerows, by rivers and streams, alongside animals and even a few people. However, just over two hundred years ago, life began to get very difficult for them."

Harold banked right round a lamppost. Rowan gripped on tighter, straining to hear above the wind.

"People started building smoke-spewing factories that choked fairy lungs, and constructed cities that destroyed many of the places where they lived. And in the cities lived cats and foxes that would prowl the streets and hunt down any fairies they could find. The fairies that were left in London sought refuge in the only green spaces that remained, but the danger was never far away. Mind your heads, please."

"What? Whoa!" Rowan and Aiken ducked as they

flew beneath a huge stone archway that stood on a giant traffic island in the middle of the road.

Rowan turned and saw Aiken looking nervous. His eyes widened as they reflected the bright headlights of the cars that sped beneath them. Harold continued, unruffled.

"That is, until one great fairy saved them all from certain destruction. She was the fairy we now call the GodMother. And not only was she a fairy, but she had the rare power of *transformation*. At that time she had taken the form of a green parrot belonging to the Duchess of Kent."

"She what?" said Rowan.

"You mustn't keep interrupting. There's a lot to explain, and not a great deal of time to do it in," replied Harold. Aiken tapped Rowan on the shoulder and rolled his eyes, and Rowan had to bite her lip to stop herself from laughing.

"As I was saying. She became very friendly with the lonely young daughter of the duchess, who lived in Kensington Palace and whose name was . . . Princess Alexandrina Victoria."

"Who?"

"What *do* they teach you at your school? Princess Alexandrina Victoria—who grew up to be *Queen Victoria*."

Rowan still felt none the wiser. "We've only got as far as the Egyptians."

"Oh, it doesn't matter," said Harold. "What's important is, the princess and the parrot became so friendly that the GodMother revealed her true identity to Victoria. Not only that, but she explained the fairies' terrible plight. So when Victoria became queen, she swore to protect all fairies in London by fencing off great swathes of land from the dangers of the city. She created her Royal Parks around the gateways that bring fairies into our world."

"What gateways?" asked Rowan.

"The ancient weeping beeches," replied Harold. "The clue's in the name. Those who feel unloved when they weep beneath a beech at the magic hour wake up as a fairy. I thought we'd covered that?"

"You should really pay more attention," said Aiken with a wink.

"Sorry," said Rowan. "It's quite hard to take it all in. Please do carry on."

"Over time fairy tribes formed around the flora and fauna that lived and grew in the parks. The Fairies of the Beast in Regent's Park, the Tree Fairies in Hyde Park, the Fairies of the Deer in Richmond Park, the Fairies of the River in Bushy Park, and so on. By day, beautiful spaces for her people, but closed to the public at dusk so the fairies could come out in peace at night. Humans call them the Royal Parks. We call them the Fairie Realms."

"What happened to the GodMother?"

"When Victoria moved house from Kensington Palace to Buckingham Palace, she created a special sanctuary for the GodMother and all the Fairies of the Birds in St. James's Park, right outside her front door. Which is where the GodMother lives to this day."

"You've left out a rather important set of fairies," said Aiken.

"I don't think we need to go into that now," said Harold.

"The ones he doesn't want to tell you about," said Aiken, leaning forward to whisper loudly into Rowan's ear, "are the ones that nearly *ate* you. The Fairies of the Fox in Greenwich Park."

Harold cut him off. "Not now, Aiken."

Rowan felt like she was in the world's most intense history lesson. "So, Harold, what about you? Are you a fairy, or a bird, or a fairy that looks like a bird? I might be getting a little lost."

"I'm just a bird, Rowan. Blessed with the power of speech by the GodMother when I was but a chick."

"Right," said Rowan. "This place just gets stranger."

"Oh, that's the best thing about it," said Aiken. Though, as she turned to look at him, she saw the smile fall from his face. She glanced over to where he was looking. A dark shape loomed out of the darkness. It was a flock of large crows swooping toward them.

"Er, friends of yours, Harold?" she asked.

The robin glanced back over his wing. "Not friends of anyone, I'm afraid. Hang on!"

He banked sharply left and then right between the trees lining the road, but the crows were not going to be put off that easily. Rowan gripped on to Harold's neck to stop herself being swung off. Harold was flying as fast as he could, but the crows were gaining on them. The great black birds made rasping, cawing sounds as they swooped in from either side. Rowan saw the glint of a crow's eye as the bird snapped its beak just centimeters from Aiken's back. He quickly shuffled up as close as he could get to Rowan and held on tight.

"Do something, Harold!" Aiken shouted.

A car was racing down the road toward them. Harold dived straight at it.

"Not that!" Aiken yelled even more loudly.

At the last moment Harold pulled out of the dive and swooped across the roof of the car, but the larger crows were chasing too fast to react—their bodies smashed into the windshield, and they spun, dazed, to the roadside.

Rowan gave Harold a reassuring pat on the neck as they glided past Buckingham Palace, over a red-jacketed Queen's Guard standing watch, and banked right into St. James's Park.

"Didn't doubt you for a second, old friend—" Aiken was saying, when out of nowhere something crashed into them with such force that it threw Rowan and Aiken from Harold's back and sent them sprawling to the ground. Their wings caught on branches as they plummeted through a tree, spinning them into somersaults before they hit the ground with two thuds.

Dazed, Rowan lifted her head to see Harold slam into the trunk of a tree before rolling to the ground in a whirl of feathers. They all slowly came to and looked around to see what had hit them. An enormous coal-black head swung out of the darkness, snapping and hissing on the end of a huge snakelike neck that weaved left and right. Rowan and Aiken scrambled for cover behind a sapling.

"Dragon!" shouted Aiken, cowering behind Rowan.

Rowan peeked out around the trunk. She saw black feathers and the arc of huge, graceful wings.

"It's just a swan, Aiken," said Rowan, breathing hard. "A black swan."

"Oh, that's fine, then," Aiken hissed back. "Just a giant, angry, bad-tempered swan. It'll be *no* trouble at all."

The swan had turned its attention to Harold and was closing in fast. The robin tried to move, but his wing was jutting out at a strange angle, and he was flapping helplessly on the ground. The swan lowered its head to strike.

"Aiken, do something!" shouted Rowan.

"Me do something?" said Aiken. "What kind of something?"

"Your sticks!"

Aiken pulled the sticks out of his belt and hurled them toward the swan. They bounced harmlessly off its feathers, but the swan clearly didn't like things being thrown at it. It raised itself up to its full height and flapped its wings, swinging its head toward Aiken with a malevolent squawk. "No. Sticks. Left," hissed Aiken, pulling up a leaf to shield himself.

Rowan let out a frustrated cry. It was up to her, then. She tried not to think about how scared she was and clawed up two handfuls of broken leaves and dirt. She threw them into the air to distract their attacker, running toward the swan and screaming as loudly as she could.

The swan looked puzzled at this tiny girl fairy thing jumping up and down in front of it. Then it rushed at her, hissing, about to strike, when . . . "Stand down, Cygnus," came a voice from somewhere.

The swan stopped dead in its tracks, twisting its long neck to look behind it. Out of the shadows came a fairy. This one was slender, graceful, and wearing a fitted robe of tiny pure-white feathers that made her look like a miniature white version of the bird that had attacked them. She didn't seem too impressed by the dirty girl fairy covered in bits of leaf. She looked Rowan up and down as if she were ever so slightly disgusted by her.

"What are you doing crashing into my swan, Oak-wings?" the fairy asked as she stroked the swan to calm it down.

The silence stretched between them, until Harold climbed stiffly to his feet. "Good to see you again, Olor."

Chapter Five

THE REALM OF THE FAIRIES OF THE BIRDS

Aiken threw his protective leaf to the ground. "We have come," he proclaimed grandly, "to see the God-Mother."

Olor ignored him. She turned to Harold instead. "How do you know my name, robin?"

"You're too young to remember. Please take us to the GodMother. We need to speak with her urgently."

Olor narrowed her eyes, and Cygnus the swan loomed behind her.

"How do I know you're not Vulpes in disguise?"

"Who's Vulpes?" asked Rowan.

"Nice try," replied Olor. "But that's exactly what Vulpes would say."

"Let us take the test," said Harold.

"The test?" asked Rowan and Aiken in unison.

Olor stared at Harold. He didn't blink.

"Follow me, then, Oakwings." She whirled around and strode back into the gloom, with Cygnus loping behind. She didn't wait to see if they were following. Aiken chased after her.

"Why does she keep calling us that?" said Rowan, her gaze following Olor and Aiken into the darkness.

"The different fairy tribes all have nicknames for one another."

"Is that why Aiken calls you 'beak face'?"

"No, that's more because he's rude."

"Oh," said Rowan. "Can you walk with that damaged wing?"

"I'll be fine," he said. "Let's go."

Eventually they caught up with Olor. She led them to a large lake in the middle of the park, teeming with waterfowl.

"Tell me which bird is the GodMother, and you can speak with her," proclaimed Olor. "You have one guess. If you fail, Cygnus will . . . take care of you."

The swan hissed with menace. Harold stepped forward.

"Not you, robin." Olor pushed him back. "She chooses."

"I really don't think I can," replied Rowan nervously.

Aiken pushed forward and spoke to Olor in a loud whisper. "Listen, the girl here hasn't got the first clue. She's literally only been a fairy for about five minutes. We're just trying to do a good deed here, get the girl where she wants to be, and then we can all go home. So let me pick out your GodMother, and we can have a quick chat and wrap this thing up."

Olor ignored him again. "The slightly smelly fairy chooses."

"Okay, now that's not necessary," said Rowan, stung. "I'll do it, then."

Aiken tried to hold her back, as if to say *I'll handle this*, which only wound her up even more.

"I said, *I'll do it*," said Rowan through gritted teeth.

Taking a breath, she squinted out into the gloomy lake. By the light of a nearby fountain lit from beneath, she took in the size of the task. The water was full of birds. Geese, swans, outrageously-colored Mandarin ducks, even pelicans. More than she could count. She didn't have a clue which one could be the GodMother.

Aiken whispered rather too loudly into her ear, "Think 'friend of *royalty*,' right? Glamorous-looking, that kind of thing."

There were certainly all manner of brightly-colored birds out there. The glow of the fountain glinted off one duck whose feathers were practically all tinged with gold. *Surely that must be the one?*

"Rowan, you don't *see* the GodMother. You *recognize* her," whispered Harold into her other ear.

"No conferring!" yelled Olor.

Rowan turned away from the golden duck. She was more confused than ever. Her eyes first fell on a great white swan, and then a grand pelican. How was she supposed to just "recognize" the GodMother? She turned away from the lake, unsure what to do. She sensed the others watching her closely.

"Whenever you're ready," said Olor, folding her arms.

Rowan turned back to face the lake. A gust of wind blew spray from the fountain across their faces.

Rowan closed her eyes, turning her face to the sky and feeling the droplets speckle her cheeks, just as her mother had turned her face to the rain by the weeping beech those seven years before. Rowan took a deep breath and let her shoulders drop. When she opened her eyes, she was looking directly at a little brown duck by the water's edge, shepherding a row of chicks up onto the bank. One of the chicks kept slipping down the bank, so the brown mother duck turned and let the chick jump onto her back to climb the slope. It was as if someone had turned on a light in Rowan's head.

"That one," said Rowan. "The little brown duck just there."

The duck suddenly dived beneath the surface of the water and disappeared for what seemed like an age. The ripples gradually stilled. Aiken slapped his palm to his face in annoyance, and Rowan shifted from one foot to the other. Beside her Harold nodded his head.

Suddenly the surface of the lake broke and a shape burst out, spinning as it went, with crystal droplets of water flying in all directions. As the shape turned in the air, it seemed to transform, its body lengthening, limbs growing, and human features emerging from beneath the feathers. It was no longer a brown duck but a fairy, glowing from within like the fountain. *The GodMother.*

Aiken patted Rowan on the back. "Never in doubt."

Olor rolled her eyes and flopped onto the ground.

The GodMother hovered just above the water's surface, sending ripples out across the lake. She wore a great cloak that shimmered in deep shades of blue, cream, and brown, rising up to a rich green hood that shone like the head of a mallard duck. Rowan took a step back in awe. But then a rustling in the trees made her spin around. She turned to see hundreds of feathered fairies in all manner of colors and plumage slowly appearing from behind nearby bushes and trees. Their eyes met hers as they rose into the air as one, each pair of wings making a violin sound that together made up a beautiful harmonic chord, like an orchestra tuning up before a performance.

"It's good to see you here, Harold," said the God-Mother.

Harold bowed his head.

"We've come to bring you a restless soul, God-Mother," said Harold, nudging Rowan forward with his beak.

"I need to get home," said Rowan quietly.

The GodMother hovered near to Rowan, beckoning her closer. She held out a hand to cup Rowan's cheek. A faint glow passed around Rowan's body, and all tension left her.

"You're safe here, you know that?"

Rowan nodded.

"But still you want to return?"

Rowan nodded again. The GodMother spread her arms wide as if conducting the orchestra of fairies that surrounded her.

"My children," she said to the fairies. "You all wept beneath the beeches. You all felt unloved."

Rowan looked around at hundreds of tiny heads, all nodding in agreement.

"But now, do you feel loved? Do you want to stay?"

The fairies nodded vigorously, and their wings beat the air more quickly, until the music rose to a deafening crescendo. Some fairies flew even higher, looping and turning in the air. The GodMother turned her gaze back to Rowan as the music died away. Rowan felt a comforting warmth on her face.

"It's all right to be sad, my child. There's always something that we miss. But this? *This* is a magical place, unlike any other you have known."

Rowan looked around at the smiling fairies willing her to like it here too.

"But do you know the best thing about it?" continued the GodMother, drawing even closer. "We all understand how you feel."

Rowan could almost sense the GodMother looking deep inside her. For the first time since she'd found herself in this place, she felt a small ache of connection. But quickly she remembered the look on Dad's and Willow's faces as they'd left the apartment that morning. One muddled and lost, the other trusting and innocent. They weren't perfect, but they were her family. And she missed them. More than anything.

"GodMother," she began. "Thank you. Thank you for your welcome. But I made a terrible mistake. I know I shouldn't be here."

The GodMother looked deep into her eyes. Finally she spoke.

"Mistakes don't occur that often," admitted the GodMother, straightening back up. "But happen they do." She looked long and hard at Harold as she said this. Her voice grew firm. "None of this changes one simple fact. You are here to stay." She began to fly back toward the center of the lake.

"What about the Heart of Oak?" Rowan called after her.

The GodMother paused in midair and turned back round. Her face was pale beneath the moonlight.

"If the Heart of Oak is real," she replied, "fairies shouldn't go looking for it. The last one who thought she'd found it was never seen again."

"Because the fairies would become human?"

The GodMother dropped her gaze. "I'm afraid not."

"I would still like to try. Please help me, God-Mother?"

"I can feel the hurt in you, little one. It's a pain I know only too well. Harold did the right thing in bringing you here. We will care for you. In time the thing that hurts you will get smaller and smaller, until you hardly know it's there. I promise."

Rowan's heart sank as the GodMother rose back

up into the air, turning out over the lake to be followed by the hundreds of Bird Fairies, shifting and swarming in the sky like a cloud of starlings at dusk. Rowan stood on the bank of the lake, feeling very alone. She felt a hand on one shoulder, and a feathered head nuzzling into the other. Aiken and Harold were standing on either side of her.

"I thought you said she was the answer, Harold?" said Rowan.

"I'm afraid . . ."

"It is what it is?" Rowan sighed.

"I'm afraid . . . I was wrong," Harold corrected her. "When my wing is healed, I'll take you back to Hyde Park. I'm sorry we came all this way for nothing."

Rowan gazed helplessly out across the lake. Hyde Park was no better than here as far as she was concerned. Neither of them was home. But for now at least, it didn't seem like she had a choice.

"Come with me," said a voice behind them. "I'll take you to our shelter." It was Olor, sitting astride the black swan's neck. She held out her hand, offering to help Rowan climb aboard. A tiny smile of sympathy crossed Olor's lips. Rowan nodded her thanks and took Olor's hand. Aiken followed after, turning to look at Harold.

"Joining us?" he said.

"Birds shouldn't fly on other birds," replied Harold.

"What about birds that can't fly?" said Aiken.

Harold cocked his head sideways, seeming to accept the logic. He hopped onto Cygnus's back.

"How am I supposed to hold on?"

But Olor wasn't waiting to find out. She dug her heels into the swan's sides, and it jerked forward. Rowan grabbed on to Harold to stop him from falling off as the swan whistled down the bank, running across the water's surface briefly before it took off into the sky.

* Chapter Six *
HOW CHICKS LEARN TO FLY

The great swan beat its heavy wings to carry them up and over a little tree-covered island before it swooped down again to splash to a halt in the water by a huge weeping beech on the other side of the lake. Olor guided Cygnus across the water toward the tree, before pulling back the branches like a curtain and showing them inside.

Beneath the great beech's canopy were the hundreds of fairies that had followed the GodMother. At the water's edge was a bonfire that reflected sparks of light off the lake's ripples, and around the fire the fairies whirled in an airborne dance. Most fairies spun as couples, orbiting the fire as their wings played music to accompany their movements. And at the center of it all was the GodMother, laughing and reeling around like a conductor dancing to the music they were creating. Aiken grinned and jumped off the swan's back, turning to Olor with his arm outstretched.

"Dance with me, Featherwing?"

Olor rolled her eyes. She slid down the swan's neck and whisked past Aiken into the crowd. Aiken smiled and chased after her. A multicolored fairy thrust an acorn cup of sweet-smelling liquid into Rowan's hands as Harold leaned over to shout into her ear above the fairy music.

"Are you all right?" asked Harold.

Rowan shrugged and tried to smile, but she sensed she wasn't really fooling her new friend.

"What about dancing? Might make you feel better?" he suggested.

"I'm not very good with dancing," said Rowan, pointing at her legs. "These things never seem to do what I want them to."

At the other side of the bonfire, Rowan could see that Aiken had finally convinced the reluctant Olor to dance with him.

"Yes, well, I have a similar problem," said Harold, shuffling his spindly claws in the dust and trying to wiggle his tail around. He looked ridiculous, and Rowan burst out laughing. Harold winced a little when he realized his wing still hurt, but he still managed to tilt his head affectionately toward Rowan.

"Okay, I can't help you with the dancing, but there is something I'm expert at. Come with me."

Rowan followed Harold out through the beech branches to a clearing in the small wood. Unable to fly with his damaged wing, he hopped up onto a low-hanging branch, ripped a few leaves off with his beak, and let them flutter to the ground below to form a soft pile.

"Okay, come up here."

She was a bit suspicious but scrabbled up the tree trunk to edge along the branch until she was perched next to Harold.

"So," he began, "when chicks learn to fly, it's pretty simple. They don't have a lot of time to worry about it. Their mothers get them out of the nest, sit them on a branch, and . . ."

Rowan yelled as Harold pushed her off the branch.

"Oof!" She hit the ground with a thump, just missing the soft pile of leaves that was intended to break her fall.

"Hmmm. That wasn't how it was meant to work," Harold said, puzzled.

Rowan brushed herself off and shot him an angry look. "What was *that* for?"

She stood with her hands on her hips. "If you want something done right," she said, "you have to do it yourself." She found some downy feathers and made a larger, more comfortable-looking pile of them beneath the branch, before climbing back up the tree.

"Move along, please."

Harold shuffled aside. Rowan raised herself up, tall and straight, flexed the muscles in her back, and stretched out her wings. She took a deep breath in and sprang into the air like a diver from a springboard. Her wings buzzed, but rather than making the same awful sound as before, out sang a single, clear, beautiful note. She gently glided toward the ground as a big smile spread across her face. She was really doing it! However, she didn't quite know how to land just yet, and hit the ground too quickly, tripping over and landing flat on her face.

"Okay. Need to work harder on that bit," she said under her breath. She turned to see Harold up in the branch looking particularly proud. "So. What else can you teach me?" she asked.

Aiken and Olor collapsed into a feathery seat, tired from dancing.

Olor took a dainty sip from an acorn cup. "What happened to your friends?"

Aiken realized he had forgotten all about them.

"Oh, you know. Rowan's only just become a fairy. It's all new to her. Probably needed to take a little time out."

"Sure. It doesn't bother you, then? Being away from all the other Oakwings?"

"Me? No." He puffed himself up. "I'm kind of what you would call a *born adventurer*."

Aiken turned away from Olor so he could stare moodily into the distance, and found himself looking straight into Cygnus's beak.

"Agh!" he screamed.

"Shall we go see what the others are up to?" asked Olor, with a badly disguised smirk.

"Sure. Yep. Why not."

Olor led Aiken out through the branches. In the nearby clearing Rowan was swooping and soaring through the branches like she'd been flying all her life. Aiken's mouth dropped open.

"Best keep that shut," said Rowan as she whizzed past, making the bangs of his hair fly up. "You never know what'll fly in."

Olor looked a little annoyed. "Not bad for a scruffy Oakwing. Why don't we have a race?"

"Race?" said Rowan and Aiken at the same time.

"Sure. Just to the flagpole on Buckingham Palace. Super-easy."

"I don't think she's ready for—" Harold began.

"Of course," said Rowan, cutting him off. "Love to."

Harold leaned in to whisper to her. "You've only just stopped landing on your face, Rowan."

"I'm going to show her what a scruffy Oakwing can do."

Harold shot Rowan a long look before stepping back out of her way. "Who's going to start us off, then?" Rowan asked.

"Go!" shouted Olor, shooting off like a rocket and taking the other two by surprise.

"What happened to 'ready' and 'set'?" yelled Rowan as she and Aiken sprang off in pursuit.

The three fairies whipped along the surface of the lake like swallows in summer, Olor stretching out in the lead, with Aiken close behind. Rowan gritted her teeth as she tried to catch up. Olor and Aiken took turns showing off, with Aiken spiraling under a footbridge as Olor looped over the top of it upside down. Rowan had plenty of determination but not enough skill, and narrowly missed the tail of a duck that squawked off in a flap. As she turned in the air to apologize to the bird, she took her eye off where she was headed and careered into an overhanging branch by the side of the lake, dropping like a stone into the water below.

"Can't! Swim!" gurgled Rowan as she struggled to keep her head above the water.

Aiken heard her shout and spun round. There was no time for his usual joking. In one seamless motion he swooped down and scooped Rowan out of the water, and deposited her on the bank of the lake. They both lay there, Rowan rubbing her head where she'd hit the branch and trying to get her breath back.

"Funny. I was going to suggest that you have a

bath." Olor casually fluttered down next to them. "Are we going to finish this race or what?"

"Give her a chance, Olly."

"No, I'm totally fine," said Rowan as she shook the water off her wings "Let's . . . go!"

Rowan jumped into the air. Olor looked at Aiken and smiled.

"You're not going to let yourself get beaten by *two* girls, are you?"

She shot off after Rowan. Aiken shrugged and raced after them both.

For the first time since she'd become a fairy, Rowan was starting to enjoy herself. Well ahead of the other two, she curved up away from the lake and over the trees lining the Mall—the long, straight road that led to Buckingham Palace. Olor and Aiken strained to keep up, but she was too far ahead for them to catch her. Rowan sped between the two lines of trees toward the palace. It was an incredible feeling. As she passed the shining, golden, winged angel on top of the Victoria Memorial, she relaxed into the flight, closed her eyes, and felt strangely peaceful. She rolled and spun in the air. A strange sensation came over her. It started as a tingle, like pins and needles. It soon felt like all her muscles were stronger, her senses sharper. But it was more physical than that. She felt like the actual dimensions of her body were shrinking and stretching all over. As she curved around the flagpole on top of the palace, with the sun just breaking into the sky behind it, she saw Aiken and Olor looking on with their mouths open wide, hovering mid-air. Then the stretching and shrinking sensation started again, before fading back to a tingle as she arced back toward them.

"Do you have *any* idea what just happened?" asked Aiken, his wings beating furiously behind him.

"Er, I beat you both by miles?"

Aiken and Olor looked at each other.

"You just, well . . . Just for a few seconds you . . . *transformed* into a white swallow," said Aiken.

"I did what?"

Somewhere out there in the blackness, something howled into the night.

"We need to talk to the GodMother," said Olor. "Right now."

✳ Chapter Seven ✳
A WING AND A PRAYER

Rowan, Olor, and Aiken snored quietly, hidden out of sight, bundled up in a bed of downy feathers in a duck house on the lake. Beyond their shelter the sun was beginning to set again toward the end of a bright summer's day. Humans were striding across the park wearing sneakers with their office clothes, keen to get home. If they had bothered looking over at the duck house on its island, they might have seen a small brown duck talking to a robin by the door.

"She has the gift, then?" asked Harold.

"Her pain is real," replied the GodMother. "I could feel it."

They glanced back inside at the sleeping Rowan.

"She won't rest easily. It's why I had to bring her," said Harold. "It reminds me of . . . the last time."

Rowan turned in her sleep. The acorn pendant that had been tucked beneath her dress fell out across her collarbone. The GodMother's eyes widened.

"What's that? Around her neck?" she asked.

Harold hopped in to take a closer look.

"Oh my," he said. "I can't believe I didn't notice before."

The GodMother lowered herself next to Rowan, slowly morphing back into a fairy as she did so. The feathers of the GodMother's wing shrank away to reveal a hand that gently lifted the pendant to her face so that she could examine it more closely.

"This changes everything," said the GodMother. "We must wake her as soon as dusk has fallen. Has she encountered a fox yet?"

Harold looked at the ground and nodded. The GodMother sighed.

"Then they will almost certainly come tonight, and she cannot be here when they do. You have to get her away, Harold. And there's only one place she'll want to go."

Harold looked troubled.

"I know you don't believe you can do this," said the GodMother. "But I do. I always have."

Rowan was dreaming. It was a dream she'd had many times since her mom had disappeared. She would open the door to their apartment to hear music. Drawn to the sound, she would slowly follow it to the living room to see her mother standing by the window. Her mom would be facing away from Rowan, with her violin to her chin, its bow sliding gracefully across the strings. Rowan would call to her, but no voice would come out. Her mom wouldn't turn. Rowan would struggle to take a step toward her, but find she could no longer move. Rowan would try to open her mouth, but no words would emerge. All she could do was watch, as tears slipped down her face. And then the dream changed from the usual. She reached for her pendant to find . . . that *another* hand was holding it! She woke with a start to see the GodMother with Rowan's pendant in her palm.

"No!" she cried, shrinking back against the wall of the duck house. "What are you doing?"

"It's all right, Rowan. We just had to be sure," said Harold in a calming voice.

"Sure of what?"

"The last time we saw a pendant like that was seven years ago," said the GodMother.

"But the only other pendant like this was my mother's. . . ."

"And where is your mother, child?"

"She disappeared." Rowan's eyes widened with the realization. "Seven years ago."

"Rowan," said the GodMother, "there's a lot to tell you, and not much time to tell you in."

"She's here? Are you saying Mom is here?"

"Perhaps, yes," replied the GodMother, but she didn't look as happy as Rowan would have liked her to.

"What's the matter? Where is she? Is she all right?"

"Slow down, Rowan," said the GodMother. "Give me a chance to explain."

Aiken and Olor began to blink awake.

"You remember the story I told you—about the last fairy who thought she possessed the Heart of Oak? She was never seen again."

"That was my mom?" she whispered.

"You know why people turn into fairies, Rowan. Because they feel unloved. And for them, coming here is the most blessed relief," began the GodMother. "But other fairies . . . like you? Well, they wish they weren't here. Like I said, it's rare, but it happens. And those fairies, those restless souls, are the ones who seem to have the power of transformation. They can transform themselves into the many plants or creatures of their Realms."

"Like Rowan can?" Aiken piped up.

"It's possible," said the GodMother.

"Like my mom?" asked Rowan.

"If the fairy I knew was indeed your mother," replied the GodMother, "she was a fairy with great power."

"So she went looking for the Heart of Oak? To get back to us?" asked Rowan, her mind racing.

"Not exactly," replied the GodMother. "She thought she already had it."

"What do you mean?"

"Her necklace. An oak tree with a carved-out heart. But before she got a chance to find out how to use it . . ."

"What? Where is she?" Rowan was almost in tears with frustration.

The GodMother exchanged glances with Harold.

"Vulpes," said Harold softly.

Aiken and Olor looked nervously at each other.

"What's Vulpes?" cried Rowan.

"Vulpes is a fairy," said Harold, picking up the story. "An angry, vengeful, dangerous fairy."

"He fell into this world many, many years ago when he was around your age," said the GodMother. "In the human world he was heir to a great estate in Greenwich, but when his father died, he fell into deep despair beneath a weeping beech in Greenwich Park. There he became a fairy of the fox. One day he saw his uncle walking through the park, and overheard him boasting of how he had been responsible for his brother's death. By getting rid of Vulpes's father, the uncle had inherited the other man's fortune. Vulpes flew into a rage, desperate to become human again to take revenge. Ever since, he has hunted down any fairy who might possess the Heart of Oak so that he might avenge his father."

"So he wanted to find my mom?" Rowan was almost in a panic now.

"Let us say that this fairy *was* your mother," said the

GodMother in a reassuring tone. "When she fell into the Realms, she was desperate to get home. Her soul was one of the most restless we had ever seen, and that made her a truly powerful fairy. Not only could she transform into the trees of Hyde Park, but the birds of St. James as well. Vulpes heard about her pendant and assumed it was the Heart of Oak. Naturally, he wanted to take it from her. He attacked the Park of St. James, along with his tribe of foxes. We lost many fairies in that battle."

"And my mother?" pleaded Rowan, terrified at the thought she might have lost her mother for a second time.

"Vulpes managed to snatch the necklace. But he realized he couldn't use it. He wasn't the most powerful fairy in the Realms, which meant the pendant was powerless in his grasp. By the time he realized this, we'd had a chance to spirit your mother out of the park to safety," said the GodMother.

"Where did she go?"

The GodMother paused, glancing around as if the walls might have ears to hear the secret. She lowered her voice to a whisper to continue. "She transformed herself into a swan and flew to the River Fairies in Bushy Park. At Bushy there was another fairy—Jack Pike. He hid her. To this day Vulpes still can't find her. But his foxes lay siege to Bushy Park and are constantly on the prowl. She's never been able to come out of hiding."

"But *you* know where she is, right?" Rowan asked.

The GodMother looked to the floor. "We . . . have an idea."

"Perfect." Rowan shook her head in disbelief. "So what will Vulpes do if he gets to her?" Rowan looked around at the others, but no one seemed to want to meet her gaze.

"He has to make sure that *he* is the most powerful fairy in the Realms." Harold paused for a breath. "By making sure that no greater fairy exists."

"And he does that by getting rid of my mother?" Panic prickled across Rowan's skin. "I have to go. I have to help. I have to *do* something!"

No one said a word.

"What's wrong?" asked Rowan, looking across the faces that were avoiding her gaze. "I'll take the Heart of Oak from Vulpes and reunite it with my mom, and then we can all go home! Vulpes won't have to defeat her, because we won't be here anyway. It's the best news I've ever had in my life!"

"It's Vulpes, child," said the GodMother. "I'm afraid you won't find it easy to steal something from him. Especially not something so precious to him."

There was a sudden hubbub on the other side of the lake. They all rushed out of the duck house to see what was happening. Fairies were flying this way and that; birds were squawking noisily.

"You need to leave—now," said the GodMother.

"I'll go to Bushy Park," announced Rowan, turning to face the others. "At least I can start to look for my mother there." She paused and glanced at her robin friend. Harold looked down at his injured wing.

"I'm sorry, Rowan. I can't fly."

"Cygnus can take us," announced Olor.

The enormous black swan rose up from the lake, beating its wings so hard, it nearly knocked them all over. Rowan smiled gratefully at Olor through the blast of air. Olor gave her a small smile in return as she climbed nimbly up onto the enormous bird, throwing a tiny harness made of ivy around its neck.

"But how will Rowan find her mother if Vulpes has never managed it?" asked Aiken.

"Because she'll have you three with her," replied the GodMother.

Aiken puffed out his chest, jumped onto the swan's downy soft back, and pulled Rowan on behind him. They grabbed a handful of feathers each to steady themselves.

"I'm not getting back on that thing," said Harold.

"No need," replied Olor, and she whispered something to Cygnus. The swan reached out a great webbed claw, grabbed Harold, and pulled him up in her grip so that the little robin hung beneath the black swan's breast.

"Oh, perfect," said Harold.

Before he could complain any further, a pack of snarling foxes suddenly broke through the trees, ridden by fairies in rust-colored furs who glared with pale orange eyes as they careered around the lake toward Rowan and her friends. Snarling and howling, the foxes bounded toward Cygnus, scattering fairies left and right. Olor immediately whipped the ivy reins, and Cygnus lurched into a run. With the foxes snapping at her claws, the swan skittered across the surface of the lake before finally lifting up and taking flight.

"Yes!" Aiken punched the air. "Too slow, furballs!" he yelled down to the chasing pack.

Rowan smiled and breathed out to slow her heart's racing. The foxes fell farther back until they were just orange ants in the distance. Cygnus wheeled high over Big Ben's almighty clock face and turned her beak heading westward along the river to safety.

For now at least.

Chapter Eight

THE ISLAND

Olor guided Cygnus to the west, following the dark, winding path of the river. As they passed over Lambeth Bridge with its sudden rush of traffic noise, red and white lights beamed in both directions. Rowan stole a glance to her left, back to the east. Less than a mile away was home. As a human girl she could have walked there in twenty minutes. As a fairy it was a whole world away. Her entire body ached to be back there. And beyond home, farther to the east, lay Greenwich Park, where Vulpes lived—the fairy she would have to fight if her family had any hope of being reunited. The breath caught in her chest as she thought about what lay ahead.

"It's a cold wind out here tonight," said Aiken. "I'm shivering like a river fairy's toes in a frozen lake."

Rowan put her arms around him to warm them both up. He gratefully held one of her arms with his hand.

"Though they mostly don't have toes, actually. Mainly tails. But I bet those get cold too," he said quietly.

Rowan craned over to try to catch a glimpse of the robin held beneath them in Cygnus's claws. "Are you okay, Harold?" she called.

"Yeah. How are things down there, beak face?" added Aiken.

"Just wonderful," replied the bird awkwardly.

"I used to live round here, you know," Aiken suddenly announced.

"Really?" said Rowan.

Aiken pointed to where the red and white lights of cars were streaming down a highway. "Just near there."

"Don't you miss being a boy, Aiken?"

Aiken shrugged. "Being a fairy is better."

"What about your parents? Wouldn't you like to see them again?"

"I don't know where they are," Aiken replied. "I never did."

Rowan didn't know what to say to him. However bad she felt, at least she knew who her family was. At least she could picture them in her mind. She only hoped that the pictures would come to life, and she'd be able to hold everyone in her arms once again.

A silence fell between them, and together they stared out into the dark night.

At a small shooting club down by the river, a night watchman heard a noise outside. It sounded like the clatter of garbage cans being turned over. He put down his knitting, unlocked a nearby cupboard, and took out a rifle. He ventured outside to investigate. As he crept around the corner, he saw a pack of foxes under a security light tearing into some garbage bags. He raised the rifle to his shoulder, narrowed his eyes, and took aim.

"You picked the wrong night to mess with me, vermin," he muttered under his breath. But as his finger squeezed the trigger, something barreled into him from the side. He flung his arms up, and the gun fired into the night sky. A straggly fox sank its teeth into the security guard's leg. As the guard cried out in pain, more foxes emerged and joined the attack, snarling and circling the man. The security guard fell to the ground, shouting for help, but no one could hear him.

Olor patted Cygnus on the neck. "How are you doing, big girl?"

The great bird turned its head to nuzzle Olor briefly, when the sound of a gunshot rang out, followed a split second later by a thud. Rowan glanced down and saw blood starting to seep between Cygnus's feathers.

"Olor!" Rowan cried out. But as her friend turned to see what had happened, the great bird was already beginning to spiral down toward the river below. Rowan and Aiken held on tight. The wind rushed past, the world spinning around them. A flash of panic hit Rowan as through the dark she spotted foxes gathering on the riverbank. At the last minute Cygnus managed to arc her body toward the water, before she finally hit the river with an almighty splash. Rowan hugged the swan's neck.

As Cygnus flipped a spluttering Harold out of the river and onto her back, Olor slipped down the bird's neck to join them.

"What happened?" asked Olor.

"I think she's been shot," replied Rowan, showing Olor where blood was starting to pool by the bird's wing.

"It's going to be okay, big girl," Olor said, stroking the bird's neck. But Rowan could see the fear in Olor's eyes.

"It'll be okay if we don't keep floating that way," said Aiken, pointing toward the bank. The pack of snarling orange was growing.

"We need you to paddle, Cygnus," urged Olor. "Away from the bank."

Cygnus tried to propel herself away from the foxes, but she was pushing against the current and was too weak from her injury. They started to drift dangerously toward the shore. Their enemies watched intently, looking more like wild, slavering wolves than city foxes. Rowan looked around desperately, unsure whether she was more scared of the beasts on the bank or the dark water. Then she saw something on the river behind them.

"Don't fight the current, Cygnus," she said. "I've got an idea."

Cygnus turned around to let herself be carried back down the river, her head bowed with tiredness. The foxes slowly paced along the riverbank. A small island in the river began to appear out of the blackness, and the foxes howled as they realized what Rowan was planning. Everyone paddled with their hands alongside Cygnus's body to help her steer toward the island, urging one another on.

The friends scrambled up onto the island and collapsed in a heap on the shore, breathing heavily as the river rushed past.

"So, now what?" asked Olor as she slumped to the ground. "Any other bright ideas?"

"We're safe here," said Harold. "For now."

They looked across at the foxes on the opposite bank, licking their jaws.

"Trapped, you mean," replied Olor.

"I'll go for help," said Harold. "The Fairies of the Deer in Richmond Park are only a few hundred meters away across that meadow. They're no friends of Vulpes."

"What about the foxes, Harold?" asked Rowan. "You'll have to get over them first."

"As long as they can't fly, I'll be okay."

Aiken muttered under his breath, "As long as *you* can fly, you mean."

Harold ignored Aiken and continued. "And as long as they can't swim, *you'll* be okay."

"Are you sure you can manage, Harold?" asked Rowan.

Harold beat his wings, seeming to wince as he did so.

"Don't worry about me. Look after Cygnus. She needs your help."

Rowan wasn't happy. She wasn't pleased about Harold leaving them, and she was even less pleased about him flying with his injured wing but knew that it was the only way. She tried to be brave about it, and gave the side of his head a pat.

"Good luck, beak face."

Harold leapt into the air over the water and then dipped down again shakily, his lame wing tip scratching the surface of the river. Rowan rushed to the water's edge, but all she could do was will him on to safety. The foxes on the opposite bank were willing him on to danger. . . . Harold seemed to skip across the water like a flat stone, and then lifted properly into the air as a police boat appeared out of nowhere, rushing headlong toward him with its lights flashing. Rowan's heart was in her mouth as Harold narrowly made it over the top of the speeding cruiser. The foxes let their jaws hang open in expectation, but the current of hot air formed behind the boat whipped Harold up high as the boat passed, looping him over the foxes' heads into the meadow behind them. Rowan gave a little shriek of delight as he disappeared from sight, but her smile quickly faded as she saw half the foxes run after him.

"He'll be okay." Aiken put a hand on Rowan's shoulder. "He's a tough old bird."

Rowan tried to smile and turned away from the water. Olor was tending to Cygnus's wound as best she could, the huge bird's head resting against Olor's chest. Aiken was looking a little lost without his red-breasted friend. Behind them the foxes howled. And as if that weren't bad enough, it began to rain.

"We need to find somewhere dry while we wait for Harold," said Rowan. "Can Cygnus move?"

Olor nodded, and helped heave the great bird up onto her webbed feet.

"Let's stay out of sight under these trees. It won't be long before the sun is back up. Aiken, can you gather some twigs to make a shelter?"

Aiken seemed glad to have something to do that he was good at, twigs being very much his department. Rowan sat down next to Olor and Cygnus. She could see dark blood sticking together the shiny black feathers of the great bird. Olor looked worried. Rowan tried to reassure her, offering her a leaf to push against the wound.

"Hold this against the blood. It's what my dad does when he's cut himself shaving. Harold will get help and it will all be fine."

Olor didn't seem convinced. "I never had anyone before Cygnus who, who cared about me. I don't know what I would do if . . ."

"It's just her wing that's hurt," said Rowan. "She's going to be okay."

But Rowan knew how Olor was feeling. She put her arm around Olor. A tear ran down her friend's cheek.

"You're all right, you know," said Olor. "For an Oakwing."

Rowan squeezed her into a hug, and Olor smiled through her tears.

"You're getting my feathers all mucky," said Olor.

Rowan smiled, spat on her fingers, and pretended to wipe the dirt off Olor's snowy white feathers.

"Good as new."

Aiken returned with a pile of sticks as big as him, and dropped them onto the ground with a clatter.

"Feel free to have a nice rest, girls. I'll just do all the work, shall I?"

A berry bounced off Aiken's head, leaving a large purple sticky mess in his hair. Olor had another tiny fruit poised to throw at him.

"Oi, not in the hair!" cried Aiken, juice dripping down his face. Some of it ran into his mouth. "Actually, it tastes pretty good."

Rowan and Olor laughed. Somewhere in the distance a fox howled, and their smiles faded.

* Chapter Nine *
A WHITE FOX AND A BLACK FEATHER

The rain had stopped, but the dampness left behind made them feel cold in the clear moonlit night. They had built a little shelter out of the sticks and were huddled together for warmth. Aiken had kept a few sticks back and was sharpening one against the other.

"Enjoying that?" asked Olor, shivering slightly.

"You might think sharpening sticks is boring, Featherwing," said Aiken, holding the point of a stick up to admire his handiwork, "but we'll see who's laughing when the foxes come after us next time."

Rowan was more worried about their absent friend. "Shouldn't Harold be back by now?"

"He may be a stuck-in-his-ways, sort of dull, annoyingly-always-right kind of bird," said Aiken, "but he pretty much always does what he says he's going to do."

Just then they heard a small splash in the distance, and then another.

"What was that?" asked Olor.

"It's probably just ducks," said Aiken.

Rowan wasn't so sure. She hurried down to the water's edge to see where the noise was coming from. Dark shapes were moving in the water by the opposite bank.

"Harold did say foxes couldn't swim, right?" Rowan asked.

"No more than you can," replied Olor.

Aiken joined her at the shore.

"Then I guess they can't be foxes," said a worried-sounding Aiken.

Olor sprang to her feet to come alongside them. Sure enough, there were foxes in the water, headed directly for them. More of the creatures swarmed behind them.

"They've been pacing up and down for hours," said

Olor, starting to panic. "And now they decide they can swim."

"Let's get up into the trees," said Rowan.

The fairies' wings made an urgent harmonic sound as they lifted up into the branches of one of the trees on the island.

"Come on, Cyggy," shouted Olor down to the swan below them. "You can do it."

Cygnus was flapping her great wings, but they weren't strong enough to get her into the sky. Olor looked at Rowan and shook her head.

"Okay, we'll have to stop them before they get here," shouted Rowan as she sprang from her branch. Her wings worked hard as she sped through the air toward the foxes' bobbing heads. She was soon joined by Olor and Aiken, and they buzzed around the foxes like angry wasps, darting in and out. One fox became hypnotized by them for long enough that it was carried away by the current. The other foxes weren't so easily distracted, and kept heading straight toward the island. Rowan and her friends whipped around and flew back to their shelter. Aiken picked up his sharpened twigs and ran to the shore.

"Come on, then, furballs!" he yelled, holding his sticks at the ready, though his legs were shaking.

Olor and Rowan hovered above him, pulling berries off nearby bushes and throwing them like baseball pitchers at the foxes' heads, making them growl. The first fox to reach the bank rose ominously out of the river, the water slicking off its back. The creature fixed Aiken with its beady gaze as it shook off the droplets, then slowly prowled closer and closer. Then it leapt at him, jaws gaping. Instinctively Aiken jabbed his stick at the fox, but he couldn't really see what he was doing, as he'd closed his eyes tight shut. Luckily, the stick rammed into the fox's mouth, jamming it wide open. Aiken opened his eyes again to see the fox howling in pain as it tried to shake itself free of the stick wedged in its jaws.

"Take that!" he yelled, but another three foxes were climbing out of the water. Aiken hesitated, his face turning pale, as the trio of foxes prowled closer. Then he ran back to the safety of a sapling.

Rowan and Olor rained down anything they could find onto the foxes' heads. Then they heard an urgent honking sound behind them. There was a flurry of feather and fur. Something terrible was happening. A fox had slipped around the side without them noticing. Its jaws were clamped around Cygnus's neck, and the bird honked desperately as she was dragged off into the undergrowth.

"No!" shouted Rowan, giving chase, with Olor close behind. They smashed through the foliage flying only a meter above the ground, breaking through leaves and grasses, before Olor hit a branch and was thrown to the earth. But there was no time to wait for her. Rowan sped on, suddenly exploding out over the open water on the other side of the island. She could see the fox who was carrying Cygnus approaching the opposite side of the river. She darted toward it, lunging down to beat her fists against the animal's head. Cygnus's head was lolling back into the water, but the fox wouldn't let go, no matter how hard Rowan tried to make it release her friend.

The fox forged on relentlessly toward the bank, dragging the swan in the water behind it. Desperately Rowan flung her arms around Cygnus's neck and clung on. Another police boat zoomed around the island. As it raced past, its wake formed a wave that crashed over them, throwing Rowan headlong into the icy black water. She spluttered to the surface, thrashing around in a panic, to see the fox struggling to drag Cygnus onto the bank. Not only was Rowan powerless to swim after them, but she couldn't even keep her own head above the water. She began to sink beneath the surface, her arms flailing as everything cut away to silence. Silence that surrounded and smothered her. She felt her lungs bursting and panic rising, but then suddenly two hands hooked beneath her armpits and dragged her out of the water. The howls of the foxes filled her ears once more as the noise of the world above returned.

Olor heaved her out of the river.

"Cygnus!" was all that Rowan could manage to say.

"Too. Late. For her," said Olor, straining to hold Rowan up. "But not. For you."

Olor half-carried Rowan back to the island, her wet wings beating hard to propel them both through the waves, until they finally collapsed in a heap on the shore. Rowan sucked in great heaving breaths.

"Thank . . . you . . ." was all Rowan could say. Olor was staring out into the night, back in the direction that Cygnus had been taken by the fox. Her eyes were wet with tears, but she was refusing to let herself cry.

"I'm sorry," said Rowan.

Olor wrenched her gaze away from the river. "It's not your fault, Rowan."

But Rowan couldn't help feeling that it might be her fault. That she could have done more. They heard a howl on the other side of the island.

"Aiken!" said Rowan, snapping them both out of their trance. They jumped up and beat their wings to shake off the water.

"Okay?" asked Olor.

Rowan was still a little shaky, but she nodded. They sprang into the air, wheeling up over the trees. Rowan glanced over at Olor. She knew how the other girl was feeling. They were high in the air now, ready to dive back to earth. Rowan hoped against hope that Aiken would be all right. They couldn't lose someone else precious to them. And all of a sudden she was thinking about her mom, and about her dad, and about her sister. She spotted Aiken bravely fending off three foxes at once, jabbing at them with his sticks.

All the worries churned around inside Rowan.

They scraped the inside of her head till it hurt and made her stomach queasy. And as she hurtled toward the ground, she began to spin. Slowly at first, then faster and faster. She felt herself stretching, changing. It was similar to the feeling she'd had by the Buckingham Palace flagpole, but this time it was as though her muscles had expanded to twice their size. She felt stronger, bigger, angrier.

She hit the earth in a whirl of leaves and caught sight of a pair of white, furred paws in front of her. Her brain raced to catch up with what her eyes were telling her. But there was no doubt.

She was a *fox*.

A snarling, angry, pure-white fox.

Rowan bared her long fangs, raising herself up to strike. The power in her muscles filled her with confidence and strength. She leapt toward the foxes surrounding Aiken, scattering them in a blur of fur and claws. But she wasn't finished yet. She snapped at their tails, caught one in her teeth, and whirled it to the ground. The others fled back to the water as she stood over the beast. She opened her jaws wide, something inside her willing her to attack. To take revenge for what the foxes had done to Cygnus. The other creature looked up at her, whimpering. She saw the fear in its eyes and found herself raising a single clawed paw, ready to lash out. . . .

"Rowan!" came a voice from behind her. "ROWAN!" It was Olor.

Rowan shook her head clear and lowered her paw to the ground, realizing what she had been about to do. She shrank back from the fox, more scared of herself than the other animal. It scrambled away. Olor came over and gently stroked Rowan's head.

"It's over," she said.

Rowan felt her fox limbs contracting, fur dissolving, tension from her muscles releasing, until she was just a shivering fairy again, curled up in a ball on the ground.

"What on earth just happened?" Rowan asked, slowly sitting up.

"You saved me, furball," said Aiken, smiling.

Rowan looked over at Olor to see that she was holding a small downy feather in her hands. It was one of Cygnus's. She crouched down and placed the feather carefully behind Rowan's ear.

"It's all right, Rowan," whispered Olor.

Olor squeezed her into a grateful hug. When they finally broke away, out of the corner of her eye, Rowan saw Aiken quietly picking another black feather from a nearby bush, and tucking it into the little belt that he kept his small sharp twigs in.

Back across the river, the last of the foxes were dragging themselves out onto the far bank. Standing high up above them on the bank was a large grizzled fox. It threw its head back and let out a howl. For all Rowan knew, it had been there all along—watching. Its head was tinged with black and gray, and its eyes shone pale yellow in the moonlight. Those eyes suddenly fixed themselves on Rowan. The fox dipped its head, as if to say, *I know who you are.* A shiver went through Rowan's body.

"What is *that*?" said Aiken.

"That," replied Olor, "would be Vulpes."

"I thought he was a fairy?" said Rowan.

"He's a shape-shifter," replied Olor.

"I guess he knows that you're one too now, Rowan," added Aiken. Rowan shakily got to her feet and went to the water's edge. She stared back at Vulpes, her eyes burning with resolve. Through the gloom Vulpes's eyes narrowed to meet hers. Rowan felt Aiken and Olor arrive at either side of her, and she felt stronger still.

Out of the darkness came the sound of hooves beating through a field. The foxes scattered, ducking beneath bushes, until with a final wave of the orange tips of their tails, they disappeared completely. Vulpes gave one last look over the river before slinking away through a hedgerow, just as an enormous red stag leapt over the top, silhouetted against the moon. The fairies could just make out a tiny bird perched on one of its enormous antlers.

"Harold!" cried Rowan.

"What took you so long, beak face?" shouted Aiken.

Chapter Ten

OUTFOXED

"So, there I was with Cervus and the Fairies of the Deer . . ."

Aiken yawned. "Is this story going to take as long as the last one, Harold?"

Rowan and Olor were perched on one of the great stag's antlers, with Harold on the opposite side. Aiken nestled in the furry bed of the deer's head as the great copper-colored beast strode along the towpath by the river.

"Well, if you don't want to hear what happened . . ."

"Can we just skip to the important bit?"

"Fine." Harold looked a little annoyed. "This is Elaphus." He waved a wing at the stag. "He's been sent to help us get to the River Fairies."

"You see?" Aiken stretched himself out and closed his eyes. "Much better."

Elaphus was being bothered by a fly. He shook his head to get rid of it, but only succeeded in throwing Aiken onto the grass below. The others clung on, laughing, as Aiken dusted himself off and flew back up to the deer's head.

"We're just glad you're okay, Harold," said Rowan, her hand reaching to touch the feather behind her ear. Aiken muttered under his breath. "Oh, you're glad that *he's* okay? I'll just fight off the foxes with my bare hands, fall from the top of a stag's head . . ."

Rowan slid down and gave Aiken a big hug, shaking off her thoughts of Cygnus for a moment.

"We never would have made it off the island without you, stick boy."

Aiken puffed his chest back out again. Rowan looked up to see Olor rolling her eyes.

"Or maybe if Rowan hadn't transformed into a fox and saved you from a certain squishing . . ."

Harold looked around sharply. "Rowan transformed into a . . . fox?"

"It was actually pretty amazing," said Aiken. "First she was flying, then she was spinning, then she was snarling, and scratching, and snapping. . . ."

Harold cocked his head sideways and looked down at Rowan. Rowan could feel him staring at her, and she started to blush.

"Harold, am I a bit weird?" she asked.

"I wouldn't say that, Rowan. I wouldn't say that at all." Rowan waited for more, but clearly that was all he had to say on the matter.

Elaphus trotted along the river path, gently jogging the friends up and down on his back. Rowan looked over to see Olor gazing at the moon glinting off the Thames.

"Are you all right?" Rowan whispered.

Olor nodded, but Rowan could see that the events of the night were catching up with her.

"Hey, Olly, look at this!" Aiken was now standing on top of one of the antlers, pretending to surf. Rowan and Olor smiled at each other. They didn't need to say a word to know what the other was thinking. *What an idiot. But kind of a sweet one.*

"Are we nearly there yet, beak face?" Aiken called over to Harold, who was perched on the opposite set of antlers.

"Not far," came the reply. "But not easy, either."

"It is what it is," Rowan said, trying to do her best impression of Harold, and making Olor giggle.

Harold didn't join in the laughter. "Vulpes could return at any time. He's seen you shape-shift. And we know how much he hates other powerful fairies. He'll try to get to you before we reach the park. He's just waiting for the right moment. And between here and the park it's not just foxes we have to worry about."

"Thanks, Voice of Doom," said Aiken.

Harold ruffled his feathers, but, as if to prove his point, when they finally cleared the tree line, they saw a riverside pub up ahead. Three men were standing outside, staring out over the river. There was no way of walking behind them, and these men wouldn't miss a stag, three fairies, and a talking bird if they wandered past. Elaphus paused and held back in the gloom for a moment. It looked like they would just have to wait for the men to leave.

"Okay," announced Aiken. "I've got this."

"Whatever you're thinking, I can guarantee it's not a good idea," replied Harold.

"Oh, you always say that, beak face. Wait here."

Before anyone could protest, Aiken buzzed away toward the pub. He skimmed along the surface of the river like a dragonfly, keeping out of sight beneath the riverbank, before coming to a halt just above the water near where the men were standing. Rowan realized she was holding her breath as Aiken buzzed his wings, sounding an unexpectedly beautiful melody.

She watched as one of the men wandered over to the river to try to work out where the sound was coming from. His mouth dropped open as Aiken rose slowly from beneath the riverbank to hover in the air, just above the water.

Rowan could see what Aiken was trying to do. If he could distract the men by the river's edge, the rest of them could sneak past.

"Go on. Both of you," she whispered, willing the other men to join their friend. But they were still deep in conversation, and neither of them moved.

Aiken looked over to his friends and shrugged, as if to ask what he should do next. Rowan made a spinning motion with her hands, and Aiken nodded before doing an impressive loop-the-loop.

The first man looked at the bottle in his hand, then

looked back to Aiken. He slapped himself in the face, before turning back to his friends.

"You *have* to see this," he whispered.

The two friends joined him, hypnotized by Aiken's aerobatics. The coast finally clear for the others to creep past, Rowan quietly urged Elaphus on. Once they were safely on the other side of the pub, Rowan waved her arms at Aiken to get him to join them. But he had a mischievous look in his eyes. He slowly flew farther out into the river, drawing the men in a trance toward him.

"Tinker Bell!" one of the men whispered in awe, almost eye to eye with Aiken. "Is it time to go to Neverland?"

Harold was so embarrassed, he couldn't look. "Come on, Aiken!" he hissed. "We don't have—"

But Aiken wasn't finished.

"Yes, Peter Pan," he said in a high voice. "Fly away with me!"

The men's feet were right on the edge of the riverbank now. They held out their arms, and Rowan thought they were trying to steady themselves. But instead they began flapping them, as if they could fly.

Then they teetered forward and crashed into the water below. Aiken began laughing loudly, but his laughter was cut short when a sudden splash of water from the men soaked his wings. He darted over toward the riverbank, flying jerkily with his sodden wings, before landing in a puddle. Rowan and Olor couldn't stop laughing. Harold was less impressed.

"Show-off," he said. "Come on, Aiken. This is no time to be splashing around."

The men thrashed about in the water, dragging themselves back toward the river's edge. Aiken shook the water off his wings and began to fly back to his friends. Rowan saw a huge orange shape loom up out of the darkness behind Aiken.

Before she could cry out, a fox grabbed Aiken from behind. His jaws latched on to Aiken's belt of twigs, and Rowan's friend gave a yelp of shock. The fox dashed through the stag's legs, carrying a struggling Aiken.

Harold was after the fox in a flash, jabbing at its head with his beak, but he couldn't loosen the fox's grip. A shake of the fox's head batted Harold off to the side, rolling him across the ground and catching his injured wing.

"Elaphus, let's go!" shouted Rowan, jumping onto the deer's head and spurring it into a headlong gallop down the riverside path after Aiken and the fox. They clattered along the path, sheltered by trees and bushes from the houses nearby, but then the fox swung sharply to the left down a narrow path toward the bright lights, cars, and people. Elaphus slid to a stop as Harold caught up, shaking off his painful fall.

"We can't follow them through there," warned Harold. "People wouldn't give a city fox a second look, but a deer? In the middle of the town? It's too dangerous."

"We can't just let them take him!" Rowan gasped. "What will they do to him?"

"There's nothing we can do, Rowan. It is what it is." But Harold couldn't meet her eye.

Rowan's hurt turned to anger. She wasn't going to let a fox do something terrible to another one of her friends.

"No, Harold, it isn't. There is *everything* we can do. Come on, Olor."

Olor jumped up behind Rowan, hanging on to the stag's antlers as Rowan shouted into his ear, "Let's go!"

The stag took off like a shot down the pathway, leaving a stunned Harold in their wake. The path became a road that wound under a railway bridge. A train rattled overhead. Bursting out from under the bridge, they were met by the sound and fury of a huge intersection, with four lanes of traffic zooming in opposite directions. Rowan felt fear and panic rise in her, but she steeled herself. There was a job to do.

She spurred Elaphus on, clinging tightly to him to keep from being blown off his back by the slipstream from passing cars. Rowan raised her head as best she could and caught sight of the fox loping across the roadway. He slipped through the great glass doors of a shiny shopping center, just as a security guard was emerging. The guard's mouth dropped open as the fox raced between his legs.

Elaphus tore after the fox, forcing cars to brake and swerve out of the way. As the stag sped past the security guard, Rowan smiled apologetically and then glanced over her shoulder. Harold was following them, but by this point the guard's legs had buckled beneath him and he'd sunk to the ground, his head in his hands.

He didn't even notice the small robin as it whisked past him.

Elaphus ducked his antlers down and burst through the doors of the mall. His hooves careered across the dimly lit marble floors as the group chased after Aiken and the fox. The shopping center would have seemed impressive to Rowan at the best of times—four empty nighttime floors of shops, glass, and escalators, with an arched glass roof that stretched its entire length. Now that she was fairysize, it was like riding through a polished white grand canyon. The fox paused, turned to snarl at them, and then scurried away, nimbly leaping from stairs to display units, easily negotiating the slippery surfaces. But for Elaphus it was an obstacle course. Rowan tried to guide the stag as best she could as he slid around elevator shafts, stairways, and benches. Then all of a sudden the fox seemed to disappear into thin air. Elaphus skated to an abrupt halt.

"There!" shouted Olor, pointing to the floor above. A flash of orange reflected against the ghostly white of the marble.

"We have to go up, Elaphus!" cried Rowan, urging

him up the steps. The stag's hooves were not built for stairs, and he scrabbled and slipped and crashed into the walls, throwing Rowan and Olor violently from side to side.

"Wait for us here," Rowan urged the great beast, and she and Olor soared up into the huge atrium. They spiraled around the walkways that stretched up the height of the building. Rowan looked anxiously for any sign of Aiken and the fox.

"There!" Olor whispered, pointing up.

On a glass-walled stairwell jutting out into the airy space at the top of the building sat the fox, its tail curled around its feet. Rowan and Olor flew up and landed on the handrail just above the creature. It was still dangling a bedraggled Aiken from its jaws. He didn't seem to be injured—that was something, at least.

"Hello, girls," he gasped. "Sorry I've been rather . . . held up." Aiken grimaced and tried to shift his body, but the fox's jaw tightened around his belt, and Aiken let out a yelp of protest.

"Let him go," Rowan demanded. "Now."

"On one condition," said a voice.

116 * *E.J. Clarke*

At the top of the stairs loomed the largest fairy Rowan had yet seen. He was as big as two fists and was clad in a fox-fleece hooded robe of deep orange and gray. Two great glossy black wings protruded from the back. It could only be . . . Vulpes.

Chapter Eleven

THE DARK FAIRY OF THE FOX

His eyes were bright but narrow, his mouth was hidden beneath a gray beard speckled with black, and his voice was dark, deep, and strangely silky—like bitter plain chocolate.

"I will let the Oakwing go. But in return you must come with me, Rowan," Vulpes said, holding out a hand to her.

"She's not going anywhere. Except to her mother," Olor said, placing a protective arm across Rowan's chest.

"Oh, I'm *entirely* in favor of organizing a reunion," said Vulpes, his voice oozing menace. He leaned toward Rowan and raised an eyebrow. "I'd like to find her again almost as much as you would."

"And then what will you do to her?" Rowan cried.

Vulpes spoke slowly and quietly.

"It really hurts that you would think I could do something . . . unkind," he said. "I only want to return something of hers."

He reached into a small pouch that was slung across his shoulders, and pulled out a necklace. He hovered closer to them, dangling it in front of them. The oak pendant. The Heart of Oak. Rowan reached out for it, but Vulpes quickly gathered it back up into his fist.

"All in good time. First I'd like to demonstrate that my intentions are entirely honorable," he said. "Would it help if I let this poor Oakwing go?"

Rowan and Olor looked at each other, surprised that it would be this easy. Vulpes hovered back to land where Aiken was suspended from the fox's mouth.

"I feel terrible about this," said Vulpes softly, picking at Aiken's chewed and mangled belt. "I simply must get you a new one."

He unfastened a strap that stretched across his own chest and lashed it around Aiken. Only, he didn't tie it round Aiken's waist; he looped it around the boy fairy's chest, pulling his wings in tight to his body so that he couldn't move them. Then Vulpes ushered the fox over to a narrow gap in the railings. The fox dangled Aiken out over the four-story drop down to the marble floor below.

"Now," continued Vulpes, "I would be only *too* happy to let him go."

"No!" Rowan and Olor cried at once.

"Well, *do* make up your mind," replied Vulpes. "This is most confusing."

"Enough," gasped Rowan, stepping toward him. "I'll come with you."

"Don't go with him!" said Olor.

Rowan raised a hand to silence her friend.

"But I need to know that my friends are safe first. Put him down and send the fox away."

Vulpes narrowed his eyes. "As you wish."

He held his hand out, and the fox pulled back from the edge, dropping Aiken in a heap onto the floor, before disappearing down the stairs.

"Get up, boy," Vulpes said.

Aiken scrambled to his feet and started toward the girls, but Vulpes caught him by the scruff of the neck.

"Not just yet . . . Oak . . . Wing," he whispered slowly

and deliberately into Aiken's ear, before turning back to Rowan. "Come down from your perch, little fairy. Wouldn't you like to see this lovely necklace up close now?"

Vulpes dangled the jewelry from a long, yellow fingernail.

"Don't trust the rusty old furball!" said Aiken, as Vulpes tightened his arm around his neck. "Just go. Both of you!"

Rowan looked at Olor.

"You go, Olor. He only wants me. I want to know you're both safe."

"You can trust me, Rowan," said Vulpes, calmly hovering up to her eye level. "Here, take the necklace; it's all yours."

Rowan didn't trust Vulpes, but she wanted to hold that pendant in her hand more than anything else in the world. She leaned out from the rail, slowly extending her arm, expecting at any moment that he might snatch it away. But he didn't. The necklace dropped into her open palm. "Stay with me, Rowan," said Vulpes, slinking back to the floor, his unblinking eyes fixed on her all the way.

Rowan looked over at Olor, and nodded. Olor hesitated, then sprang up into the air and away. Rowan lost sight of her friend as the fairy disappeared behind an exposed elevator shaft. Rowan took a deep breath and jumped down from the handrail to stand facing Aiken and Vulpes.

"Now let him go," she said as firmly as she could manage. From behind her came the sinister scrape of claws on marble. She glanced back over her shoulder. The fox was back.

"My pleasure," said Vulpes. With a sudden movement he lifted Aiken into the air and tossed him over the glass barrier, out into the void.

"No!" Rowan felt the air leave her body.

Vulpes signaled to the fox, and the creature leapt toward Rowan, its lips drawn back from pointed teeth. Rowan screwed her eyes shut, desperately trying to transform into something, anything that might fight off the fox. But nothing happened. Her powers had deserted her. Before she had time to wonder why, she felt an impact from her side. But it didn't feel like the dreaded jaws of the fox. Instead she felt the welcome embrace of a fairy's arms scooping her into the air. Rowan opened her eyes.

"Miss me?" Olor yelled as they swooped away through the gleaming building, her wings vibrating with urgent musical chords. Diving toward the exit, they were joined in the air by . . .

"Harold!"

. . . who was carrying a bedraggled fairy on his back . . .

"Aiken!"

"That midair catch isn't a trick I'd like to try again. Not much room for error," said Harold.

They swept down to the ground floor, with Vulpes's screams ringing in their ears. Elaphus was cantering toward the exit. Olor flew expertly above him and dropped Rowan onto his glossy back, before flying down to grab on to his neck. Behind them the big fox was racing down the stairs with an enraged Vulpes riding it, spurring it onward. Elaphus started scrabbling across the marble, his hooves sliding like they were on ice. Bellowing in panic, he bundled past a stunned cleaner.

Rowan glanced back. Right behind them the fox wasn't so lucky. He lost his footing and slipped into a glass wall with a huge thud as the cleaner stared, openmouthed. The fox scuttled out through the door, darting between the man's legs. Rowan could just glimpse Vulpes hanging beneath the fox's neck. The security guard from the other end of the mall arrived, his face glistening as he gasped for breath. He and the cleaner exchanged a look of disbelief.

"Did you just . . . ?" said the guard.

The cleaner shook his head.

"Good. Me neither."

Rowan felt a rush of cold air hit her body. Turning back round to the front, she saw that they'd emerged out into the street. Elaphus galloped down the middle of the road, forcing cars to swerve out of his way. Rowan ducked down and clung on as best she could. Aiken and Olor did the same. Harold's claws gripped tight into the stag's pelt. They raced across a stone bridge, and Rowan stole another glance behind them. She could see Vulpes and the fox in the distance. Streams of orange fur flooded out of side streets as, one by one, more foxes joined the chase. Soon there was a whole mass of orange chasing them over the river. It was as though every fox in London had raced to this point—and the pack was gaining on them.

"Faster!" Rowan cried.

Elaphus lengthened his stride, and as they reached the other side of the bridge, he turned sharply to the left. Suddenly it was soft earth underfoot again. They were racing through a park down a long avenue of trees. Ahead of them loomed the enormous red palace of Hampton Court.

She turned round, and her eyes opened wide as she saw a huge pack of foxes swarming down the avenue of oaks. Elaphus swung to the right again, through yet more trees, to the side of the palace and out the other side through a giant wrought iron gate. But across the road the gates to Bushy Park were shut, and they were far too tall for Elaphus to jump over.

"We have to say good-bye here, old friend," said Harold urgently, as they slid from the stag's back.

"But the foxes . . . ," protested Rowan.

"Are chasing *us*. If he runs now, they won't follow him."

"Thank you, Elaphus, thank you." Rowan sprang into the air to kiss the great stag on his soft head. "Now, run!"

The stag bellowed and galloped straight at the pack of foxes. Rowan breathed a sigh of relief as the foxes scattered and Elaphus disappeared through the trees to safety. Harold and the fairies took their chance, and slipped between the narrow iron bars of the gate.

"It's okay. The foxes won't be able to get through," Harold said, panting. Rowan felt her shoulders sag with relief. Finally she unclenched her fist to reveal her mother's pendant—the simple carved tree perfectly complementing the golden oak shape of her own acorn. It seemed like such a small thing for it to be so important. How could *this* be the key to going home? She held the pendant to her cheek as a fox scream pierced the air behind them. Vulpes's foxes crowded up against the iron railings of the closed gate, yelping and howling. At a distance Vulpes sat astride the biggest, angriest fox. He stared straight at Rowan, but he wasn't coming in. Aiken followed Rowan's gaze as she met Vulpes's eyes.

"Furball's scared," he said, by her side.

"Furball's waiting to bring an army of foxes through the gates when they open at dawn," said Harold, flying over to join them. He ruffled his feathers. "We don't have much time."

* Chapter Twelve *
THE REALM OF THE RIVER FAIRIES

Time was running out. Dawn wasn't far away. Rowan and her friends raced through Bushy Park, soaring around an elegant fountain with a golden statue of a beautiful woman. The figure gazed down at Rowan as they flew past, and Rowan remembered her mom again, looking down at her by the Elfin Oak as she read Rowan stories. A shiver of concern ran through Rowan. Would her mom still be here, in Bushy Park—and how would Rowan find where she was hiding? Would they be able to go home together? They had come so far, and yet there was still so much to do. She felt queasy and knew it wasn't because of the flying this time.

They followed Harold as he banked left to skim along the surface of a narrow winding river lined on either side by trees. They followed the river under a bridge and into a woodland filled with giant ferns and rhododendron bushes laden with deep red blooms. After passing above a network of brooks, they came to rest on a great lily pad at the edge of a large pond.

"Somewhere near here," mumbled Harold. "The entrance must be somewhere near here."

"So when the GodMother said you had an idea where Rowan's mom is," said Olor, "how much of an idea was it?"

"Couldn't she have drawn you a map?" added Aiken.

"Well," replied Harold, "our theory was that she'd be hidden near water. Because foxes don't like it much."

"*That* was your plan?" said Olor. "How do we even know she's near this pond?"

There was a pause and a cough. "We don't," Harold admitted.

Aiken groaned, then lifted up the corner of the lily pad, making them all sway in the other direction. "Nothing under here, beak face."

"It's going to be light soon, so let's get started," said Rowan.

The friends all sprang into the air and began searching around the lake for anything that could be an entrance to a secret hiding place—through ferns, reeds, and overhanging willow trees. There was nothing to be found anywhere. They flopped by the side of the lake. Rowan's body ached with tiredness, and her tummy rumbled. The ground was wet with dew, and it started to soak right through her. It had been a long night for all of them, and dawn was starting to break, with bruised streaks of light stretching across the sky. Before long the park gates would open for the day. People . . . and foxes . . . could rush in at any moment. Rowan looked all around her. Her eyes came to rest on the still surface of the pond. Rowan stood up as the first ray of morning sun twinkled behind her.

"So, why would Vulpes and the foxes have been searching all this time and still not found the way in?"

"Because they're not very clever?" asked Aiken.

Rowan ignored his attempt at a joke and continued. "What if the entrance wasn't *near* the water?

Aiken looked blank. Rowan could see he had no idea what she was talking about.

"Aiken, you said River Fairies don't have toes, they have tails, right?"

"Yes . . . ?"

"So they're not going to walk into their den, are they? They're going to swim into it."

She leapt into the air, her wings trilling with excitement as she circled the lake. She tried to peer beneath the surface of the water, but it was too murky. Instead she turned toward the sky and began spiraling higher and higher.

"What are you doing, Rowan?" shouted Olor.

"If my mom is here," said Rowan, "I'm going to find her."

As Rowan wheeled round and round, she tried not to think about the dark, forbidding water below her, nor the fact that she still couldn't swim. "I'm not scared, I'm not scared," she murmured to herself. Then she pulled her wings together tightly behind her and dived toward the lake. She closed her eyes and felt the air rush past her face, rippling her wings, as she held out her arms to a point in front of her.

"Rowan!" screamed Olor.

It was the last thing Rowan heard as she hit the freezing cold water.

Aiken and Olor rushed to the water's edge as Rowan smashed through the surface of the lake, disappearing completely from view. They waded in as far as they could get, Aiken even diving under to see if he could glimpse her, but with no success. Bubbles rose to the surface and then subsided, until the water was still again. Aiken and Olor turned to Harold.

"But she can't . . .?"

Harold didn't look at them.

"We must have faith in her. The same faith that she just found in herself."

Rowan didn't dare open her eyes as she spiraled down into the cold depths of the pond. She'd been holding her breath for so long now that she didn't even know if she could make it back to the surface. The fear began to rise in her again. Maybe this was the worst idea she'd ever had. Perhaps it would be her last. She blew the air out of her lungs as slowly as she could, until there was none left.

Suddenly she felt something brush across her leg—something scaly. Then she felt her hand being grasped. *What in the Realms holds your hand under water?* She opened her eyes. There, right in front of her, was a pale green-eyed girl, with a mane of red hair waving around her head. Rowan realized what had been brushing across her legs. It wasn't a fish's tail. It was a girl's. The girl in front of her was a river fairy.

The girl gave a brief smile and then flipped down and away from Rowan, to be joined by a group of others. They were tiny mermaid-like creatures with splodgy orange, black, and white tails like little koi carp. They had translucent fins where other fairies would have wings. Their hands beckoned Rowan to follow them.

Rowan realized that she hadn't taken a breath in well over a minute. And what's more, she didn't need to. Something was happening to her. She looked down to see her legs fusing into a shimmering, scaly tail. Her arms shrank back into her body, and she felt her wings changing shape and dissolving into fins. She was a fish—a silvery white one—turning and gliding through the water. Beside her she felt the reassuring presence of the River Fairies guiding her toward the bottom of the lake.

As the sediment cleared, Rowan could see that they were swimming toward an underwater cave. They entered the cave's dark mouth and went deeper still before shafts of light broke up the blackness ahead. She swam toward the glow and broke the surface to find herself in an air pocket of some kind. Here she felt her limbs stretch and reach out as she became a fairy girl again.

Panic took hold as she thrashed her limbs around and felt her body starting to sink back under. Then the River Fairies pressed against her, bearing her up and over to the water's edge, before whipping their tails and disappearing back under the water. Rowan lay on the cold, wet rock, sucking in big heaving breaths. "You did it," she whispered. She allowed herself a small smile before dragging herself to her feet.

Rowan was standing in a big, airy space like an ancient church built of stalactites and stalagmites. High above her head, chinks in the rock threw shafts of sunlight across the water's surface, making it sparkle and reflect dancing patterns back up the rock walls.

A boat made out of bark emerged from a dark cave off to one side. Standing up in the vessel, moving a long wooden pole through the water, was a boatman dressed in black. He pulled up alongside Rowan.

"An Oakwing, eh?" he said, catching sight of her wings. "How did you get down here?"

"Er . . . I swam."

"Fascinating. An Oakwing that swims." His eyes narrowed as he gazed into Rowan's face. He seemed to glimpse something there. "You'd better come with me."

Rowan climbed nervously into the boat and sat with the boatman at her back. She took a moment to steel herself. The boatman moved the long pole through the water, and they slowly began to glide through the cavern, heading straight for a waterfall that crashed down from a lip in the cave roof.

"Are you sure this is . . . ?"

But Rowan couldn't finish her sentence before they passed through the cascading water and out the other side. Completely drenched and starting to shiver, she beat her wings to shake off the water and warm herself up as the boat slipped down a dark, winding tunnel that was cut across every now and then by light spilling in from above. Finally it opened out into another cavernous space even larger than the first.

Rowan felt a mist of tiny droplets speckling her face. Where water spilled in through the cavern roof, it curved into shimmering, twisting, staircase waterfalls. And in the center the water rushed down, only to jet back up again in a series of elaborate natural fountains. The light cutting across the spray formed spectacular rainbows of color. This wasn't a den. It was a palace. A palace of pure water.

"Are you . . . ," Rowan began.

"Jack," he said. "Jack Pike. Pleased to meet you."

The boatman was no longer wearing black, but instead was dressed in an ornate robe of water lilies over his silvery body. And when he lifted his pole from the water, the pondweed fell away to reveal a pointed trident. He gripped it like a staff as he stepped out of the boat and onto slippery rock. Here he was, right in front of her, the fairy that Harold said had been protecting her mother. The fairy held out his hand to help her out of the boat. His webbed feet stuck to the floor, where hers slid around like they were on ice, and she clung on to him.

"I do apologize," Jack began. "Our home isn't so comfortable for outsiders, but you are most welcome here. Have you come all the way from the Realm of the Tree Fairies?"

"My friends," she told Jack. "They're stuck by the lake, and the park is about to open . . ."

"We'll take care of them; don't you worry."

Rowan wasn't sure what to make of him, but she couldn't wait any longer to ask the question that had been eating away at her insides.

"My mom," she whispered. "Is she here?"

Back up in the park, Harold, Aiken, and Olor were getting more and more concerned. The sun was even higher now, and they knew the park gates would be opening soon. It was the time of day when Aiken and Olor would normally be hidden away in treetops or tree trunks, sleeping through the danger of the daylight.

"I just want to say, Olly," began Aiken, "that if anything happens to me, I want you to have my collection of sharp sticks."

"That's a very generous offer," Olor said, not sounding too impressed. "But right now I'm more worried about Rowan."

There was a small splash over on the far side of the lake.

"What was that?" asked Harold.

Aiken flew over to investigate.

"Rowan?" he called.

He hovered as low as he could, trying to peer through the water. He turned back to them.

"No, nothing here."

Suddenly something reached out and plucked him from the air. Ripples circled out as he was dragged beneath the surface.

"Aiken!" screamed Olor, hurrying over to the water's edge.

The waters parted and up rushed Aiken, spluttering droplets everywhere.

"It's the River Fairies! I've found the way in!"

He spun round and dived back under. Olor looked at Harold with wide eyes. Harold held out his wing.

"Erm, after you?"

"No, my dear Harold, after *you*," came a syrupy voice from behind him.

Harold froze, then slowly turned round. Vulpes was emerging from the undergrowth with a pack of foxes at his sides. Astride the foxes was a gang of dark orange-and-black-furred fairies, with thin orange eyes narrowed against the dewy morning light. Harold slowly backed away from the creeping foxes, toward Olor and the lake.

He whispered under his breath, "Quick, Olor, into the water."

"Come *with* me, Harold."

"Robins and water don't mix. Now go!"

"Then fly, Harold, fly!"

Olor hesitated, then dived under the water. Before Harold could lift off, the foxes pounced on him in a whirl of fur and feather. The fairies riding the orange beasts made sure their animals kept him pinned to the ground. One of the foxes dipped a paw into the lake and whined, trying to work out where the white fairy had disappeared to.

"What's under there, Harold? Is it the way in?" Vulpes asked, and rose effortlessly up into the air. He hovered over the water, the beat of his black wings sending ripples out across the lake. Harold gasped for breath and twisted his head away.

"I said. Is. It. The. Way. In?"

"I honestly don't know, Vulpes."

"I don't believe you. And I don't like animals that lie. Where is the daughter? Where is the Heart of Oak?"

"They're both safe from you. Leave her alone."

Vulpes cried out with frustration. "Tell me, robin! And don't think I don't know who you *really* are."

"You know *nothing* about me!"

Vulpes signaled to the fairies and foxes pinning Harold down, and they slowly crushed the wing that Cygnus had injured. Harold cried out, trying to work himself loose. Then the foxes suddenly let go, leaping back and howling as a roaring sound from the lake filled the air. The bedraggled robin's wing hung limply from his side. Before he could move, a huge wave crashed over him and pulled him into the lake.

Slowly he sank beneath the surface, his wing useless to help him. Before panic could set in, he found himself cradled by a gentle shoal of River Fairies carrying him deeper and deeper. As they entered the dark cave at the bottom of the lake, his vision began to blur. The last thing he remembered glimpsing was the silver scales of a river fairy's tail. . . .

Chapter Thirteen

A FAMILY AFFAIR

Jack led Rowan up a stone staircase that led behind another waterfall, through glistening corridors, and finally into another large cave with colored crystals jutting out of the rock walls. Here and there smaller streams of water poured down from the cave roof like liquid chandeliers. In the center of the cave a clear sheet of water fell like shimmering glass into a pool below, throwing up a mist that swirled around the space.

A shaft of light illuminated a green figure behind the falling water, standing on an island of jagged rock. A wooden bridge linked the island to the main shore. Music rang out across the cave. Rowan recognized the song immediately. It was a tune that could only be played on a violin, a string of notes that she remembered from her childhood. Rowan crept closer to the pool. The sheet of cascading water made the figure flicker and sparkle.

Almost without realizing it, Rowan vibrated her wings to create a musical note that harmonized with the music she could hear. For a second they seemed to play a duet, perfectly in tune. Then the violin stopped, and the figure slowly moved behind the glimmering wall of water to emerge at one side. First came a hand holding the violin, intricately fashioned from a carved acorn cup, then another hand grasping a reed for a bow. Then a long flowing green robe of rowan leaves, and a headdress made of woven willow nestled on top of auburn hair.

"Mom," Rowan breathed. There was no mistaking the face from the photograph in Rowan's apartment. Her mother's face lit up as she swept over the bridge and enfolded Rowan in her arms, the violin and bow clattering to the ground. Rowan crumpled into the embrace. Even through her mother's robe of leaves, Rowan caught that familiar scent she had almost forgotten. A sweet smell that had long since left the clothes in the wardrobe that her dad couldn't bring himself to pack away. This was truly her mother, after all these years. As the tears started to come, Rowan slowly let out a breath. She didn't dare let go. She could feel her mother trembling. Rowan looked up into her face. Her cheeks were wet with tears. Finally her mother broke away to gaze at Rowan.

"It's not a trick, is it, Mom? It's really you?"

Her mother tapped her own chest. "It's me, Rowan." Then she put her hand on Rowan's heart. "And it's you. Just the same."

"Maybe a bit smaller than before?"

Her mother smiled through her tears. "I was thinking how much you'd grown."

Rowan reached out to wipe a fresh tear from her mother's cheek. She held her fingers against her mother's skin to feel the warmth of her. Then she felt her mother's body tense. Beyond the cavern came a noise.

"Never a moment's peace!" exclaimed Jack, breaking the spell.

"Maybe, Jack, you could go and see what's going on?" asked Rowan's mother. Her voice sounded strained, not how Rowan remembered it at all.

"What? Oh, I see. Sending me away. No Jacks wanted here."

He swept out of the cave. Rowan's mother let out a long breath.

"I've so much to tell you, Mom," Rowan began.

"I want to hear it all, Rowan," her mother said, stroking her hair. "I want you to tell me everything. Everything I've missed . . ."

"Yes, yes! There's school, there are these girls that bully me a bit, and Dad, he's, you know, he's always in his head, but we've kept your chair in the same place, and I played your violin the other day, and Willow is really sweet but a bit of a pain, and, and . . ."

Her mother may have been smiling, but Rowan could tell something was wrong.

"How are they? Willow? And your dad?"

"Dad really misses you, and I really miss you. We all miss you. . . ."

"Are they . . . happy?"

Rowan paused.

"Willow . . . ," she began, not knowing quite what to say. "She doesn't really remember."

Her mother closed her eyes.

"And Dad. He's, well, he's just not the same as he was. But you'll see for yourself, Mom! I have your necklace. The Heart of Oak! We can go home. Together."

Rowan held out the wooden pendant and looped it over her mom's head. Then she threw her arms tightly around her. The years they had spent apart melted to nothing. In their place rose a certainty that everything was going to be all right. Their family would be reunited and happy again. She looked up into her mother's face.

"I'm so glad you're here, little one," said her mother, but Rowan felt a flicker of doubt. Why wasn't her mother smiling? "There's so much I need to tell you, too."

Before she could carry on, Jack emerged from the shadows.

"It's your friends, Rowan," he said. "The bird. Seems to be hurt."

Rowan and her mother rushed to find Harold lying in a shallow rock pool carved from colored crystal. Female River Fairies swam around tending to the injured bird. A worried Aiken and Olor pulled Rowan into a hug. Rowan broke free and kneeled down to gently rest her hand on the robin's head. He opened an eye.

"Did you . . . find her?" he asked, forcing the words out.

Rowan took her mother's hand and drew her toward Harold.

"She's here. This is my mom."

Harold smiled and closed his eye again. Rowan looked up at her mother.

"He just needs to rest," her mother said quietly.

"The bird will be fine here," Jack said. "My River Fairies will look after him." He came to stand between Rowan and her mother. "Come. It's time to eat."

"What about the foxes?" asked Aiken. "They know we're here."

Jack's face clouded. "They've not found a way in for seven years," he said quickly. "We don't need to panic now."

Olor was bent over Harold, placing a pillow of moss beneath his head. She straightened up and raised her eyebrows at Rowan.

"What do you think?" Olor asked.

"He'll be fine!" insisted Jack. Before Rowan could say anything, he was already striding out of the cave.

Rowan gripped her mother's hand as they followed.

Down a tunnel, they emerged into a small but cozy cave with a crystal-clear pool. A lily pad floated in the center of the water, serving as a dinner table, full of glistening salads of watercress, steaming bowls of samphire, and acorn cups of dandelion-flower marmalade. Rowan's stomach rumbled at the sight of it, and she realized just how hungry she was. Web-footed river fairy waiters ushered the friends to sit on little stalagmite stools just under the surface of the water.

"You want us to sit . . . in the water?" said Olor.

"Yes! Make yourself at home!" said Jack.

"I've never been in a home like this before," whispered Aiken.

Rowan could have been sitting in a bucket of ice and not cared at all. She sat by her mother, and squeezed her hand tightly.

"Welcome to you all," said Jack, standing and raising a goblet of nectar. "Not since your mother fell into this world, and into my life, have I been so happy."

Rowan's mother smiled awkwardly.

"It's like having a queen by my side, and now a princess too," he continued, gazing at Rowan. She shifted in her seat.

"Finally," he said. "My very own *family!*" There wasn't anything in Jack's speech about helping them get home. Her mother clasped Rowan's hand. A team of fairy waiters brought a huge roasted piece of meat on a giant spit to the table.

"Leg of frog!" cried Aiken. Olor was looking back at Rowan to see if she was okay. But Rowan wasn't sure herself.

Rowan sat on a bed of downy feathers in a beautiful nightgown of woven flax. Aiken and Olor had gone to sleep with Harold for the night.

Rowan's mother combed the girl's hair with a brush made from a tiny fir cone. Her locks were all tangled from the epic journey they had been on, and the brush caught in them, making Rowan wince.

"I didn't mean to hurt you, Rowan," said her mother.

"It's okay, Mom. It's a bit of a mess."

"No, I didn't mean to hurt you by leaving. One

minute I was there, sitting under our tree, and the next . . . I was here."

"It's okay. The GodMother told me. You had to escape, and then you were trapped."

Her mother smiled a sad smile.

"But now we can unlock the Heart of Oak together and go home," Rowan said, turning the pendants over in her hands.

"Rowan," she began nervously. "It's so good to see my necklace again. It was the only thing I had in this world that we shared in some way, and it hurt so much when Vulpes took it away. But I have to tell you, it's just a . . . trinket. I bought this and your acorn from an antiques stall on the Portobello Road. I don't think either of them is special, other than what they mean to us."

Rowan's happiness leaked away as the words tumbled out of her. "But, but, Aiken said, the GodMother said, Vulpes said. The Heart of Oak. You unlock it and you go home. Don't you believe it's true?"

"Rowan, there's not been a minute in the past seven years when I haven't thought about going home. Thought about every possible thing I could do. Anything, even just to let you know that I was still alive. And I hadn't forgotten you. But I never found a way." She lifted her oak pendant from Rowan's palm. "Once I thought this might be the Heart of Oak. But it's just a beautiful piece of wood. I'm sorry, Rowan. I wish that weren't true."

Rowan hugged her mother, breathed her in. Then she heard her mom's voice whisper urgently into her ear.

"Because we have to find a way for *you* to get home. It's not safe for you here, little one. I can't get back, but you have to. I couldn't bear for you . . . not to be free.

Rowan pulled away.

"What do you mean, Mom? We're going to find a way together. I know it. We can be human again. Be a family again."

"You don't understand. I'm not just trapped by Vulpes, but by Jack, too."

"But he's guarding you, isn't he? Protecting you from Vulpes?"

"It began that way, yes. But he's lonely, Rowan. He doesn't want me to leave, and now that he's met you . . ." Her mom's hands twisted in her lap. "He'll want to keep you, too. You heard him—*his family*. That's how he sees us. But we can't let it happen. You have to go!"

"And leave you here as his prisoner? What about me? And Willow? And Dad?"

"Those things don't matter to him, Rowan. They're a world away from Jack. A different life."

"But don't they matter to you?" The words burst out of Rowan before she could stop them.

Her mom's voice broke. "Yes, yes, they do."

She gently pressed Rowan back into the bed and tucked a blanket over her body. Rowan was so tired, she couldn't resist. She closed her eyes as her mom pressed a kiss against her forehead.

"We'll talk more tomorrow, I promise. You must rest. Good night, my love."

Rowan hadn't been called 'my love' for seven years. She drifted to sleep in the warm feathers, hoping against hope that what her mother had said about returning home wasn't true.

A distant moaning sound woke Rowan. Her mother was asleep in a chair. The noise was coming from down the hall. Rowan gently kissed her mother, crept out of the bedroom, and tiptoed toward the sound. She passed Olor, tucked up neatly in a bed of moss, with Aiken spread-eagled near her feet, snoring gently. And then at the end of the hallway, she found Harold. He was having a nightmare. She kneeled beside him and placed a hand softly on his brow. He really didn't look well. His feathers had lost their shine, and his chest was heaving up and down far too quickly. He seemed to relax at her touch, and slowly opened his eyes. They widened at the sight of her brushed hair and nightgown.

"Oh my. I never knew you were a *girl* fairy."

"I can leave you outside for the foxes, you know."

Harold smiled, before raising himself painfully to his feet. He cocked his head to one side.

"You showed your mother? The Heart of Oak?"

Rowan nodded.

"And?"

"She doesn't think it's real."

"But it must be. Is she sure?"

Rowan shrugged.

Harold looked disappointed for Rowan, but then

seemed to rally. "But you've found her again, Rowan. That's what's important, isn't it?"

"No. Yes. Maybe. Why does it all feel so terrible, Harold? What good does it do for us to be trapped here, waiting for Vulpes to destroy everything?"

"It's not happened yet. . . ."

"Matter of time, though, isn't it, Harold? 'It is what it is,' right?"

"It's up to you to change it."

"How is that going to happen, Harold?" She held up the pendant. "If this really is just a lump of wood?"

"Because, well, you're a very special fairy too."

"Everyone keeps saying that, but all these powers don't seem to be helping me with anything that . . . you know . . . anything that really matters. I can't even control them. They just, well, happen to me."

"It wasn't the powers I was talking about. Even if you didn't have those gifts, you would still be special."

"That's very sweet, Harold," she began, "but once you get past these new tricks I can do, I don't think anything has changed."

"Oh, is that so?" Harold wasn't going to let that pass. "It took more than a trick to recognize the GodMother.

It wasn't your powers that gave you the determination to protect your friends. And yes, maybe the turning-in-to-a-fish thing helped you find your mom at last, but it was your courage that enabled you to face your fear of the water."

Rowan felt her cheeks flush red, but deep down she knew that he was right.

"Back in the Park of St. James, while you were asleep," said Harold, "the GodMother told me she believed I could help you, even though I wasn't sure. But *you're* the one who's helped me see that things can change. You're the one who's shown me that some-times, well . . . it *isn't* what it is. Nothing's impossible. Heart of Oak or no Heart of Oak."

Rowan couldn't help but smile. Quickly she kissed Harold on his feathery cheek. She snuggled in next to him under his wing, lay back, and began to drift off to sleep.

"Ouch."

"Sorry."

Rowan's mother woke to see that her daughter was no longer in her bed. She padded down the corridor, checking in all of the smaller caves, until she found Rowan asleep next to Harold.

Smiling, she leaned down to lift her daughter's hair gently out of her face, but pulled up short when she saw Rowan's wings turning white and feathered, appearing and disappearing. Rowan's whole body was alive with change. One second her legs were scaled like a fish tail, the next rough like silver birch. Her arms were feathered, then furred. Horns seemed to sprout from her head and then dissolve as quickly as they'd appeared.

Rowan's mother sat beside her and put her hand to her daughter's forehead. Rowan was hot to the touch. She stroked Rowan gently until the transformations began to slow down and then stopped altogether. Then she climbed to her feet and went to walk away down the corridor, a mixture of pride and fear etched across her face.

Chapter Fourteen

ROWAN TAKES FLIGHT

Rowan sneezed herself awake. Harold's feathers were tickling her nose. But before she had a chance to push them away and go back to sleep, Aiken and Olor appeared beside her.

"Get up, get up!"

"What do you mean?"

Harold stirred.

"It's the foxes," Olor said. "They've found a way in."

The friends rushed out of the room to find the palace in commotion. Jack was running back and forth, shouting at the River Fairies to go one way, before yelling at them again to go back the other. Rowan's mother raced over to meet Rowan and her friends.

"Follow me. Now!"

She led the friends up through the palace. River Fairies splashed around them, grabbing anything that could be used as a weapon to defend themselves.

"We'll only be able to hold him off for a short while," she said.

"What are we doing?" asked Rowan.

"My love," said her mother. "We have to get you out."

Rowan started to panic.

"No, I'm not going on my own. I've decided. If you can't leave, I'm going to stay here with you. We have to protect you from Vulpes."

"No, Rowan. We have to protect *you* from Vulpes."

"What do you mean? He only wants me so that he can get to you, and if he's inside the palace, I don't matter to him anymore, surely?"

"He is looking for the most powerful fairy in the Realms, Rowan. I don't think he realizes how much my powers have faded."

"What do you mean?"

"I've lost the power to transform, Rowan. The most powerful fairy in the Realms now is *you*."

Rowan felt her stomach drop inside her. "But that can't be?"

She turned to look at Harold, Aiken, and Olor, but they just nodded.

"Then I'll stay and fight him with you."

"It's not that simple, Rowan. Now that Vulpes has found his way into the palace, there is no place left to hide. Even if we beat him here, he will only come after you. Again and again. His anger is too strong, his foxes are too powerful—he will never rest until he finds you. You need to go, for your sake and for ours. He will destroy everything and everyone that stands in his way."

"But I've only just found you again! How am I supposed to leave you now?"

"Because I need to know that you're safe, and that you're free. And so that you can take my love to your dad and your sister, and tell them that I never forgot about them. Never stopped loving you all."

"How is she going to succeed where you and Vulpes both failed?" asked Olor.

Rowan's mother took off her wooden oak tree necklace and placed it gently around her daughter's neck.

Then she took Rowan's acorn and slotted it perfectly into the center.

"There was a hole in the heart of my necklace," Rowan's mother began, "but not anymore. Because of you, Rowan. You have it within you to do great things."

A shout came up from deep in the palace. It was Jack yelling for them to come back.

"Quickly now," said Rowan's mother. "Before Jack leads them straight to us."

The friends climbed higher through cascading staircases of water, before finally emerging into another great space. This time, however, a small circle of sky could be seen high above them. The biggest waterfall yet poured in through it and crashed past them to a large pool far below.

Beside the water beneath them, a great battle raged. Jack was swinging his trident around his head to fend off a mass of foxes. River Fairies hurled rocks at the beasts and their riders, but from the cries of desperation it was clear that the fairies weren't going to be able to hold back the attackers for much longer.

"Up here is the only other way in or out of the

palace." Rowan's mother pointed toward the hole in the cave roof. "As a fairy, the waterfall would blast you back down as soon as you got anywhere near it." She paused. "But as a bird? You could make it through. I arrived here as a swan. Perhaps *that* is the way you can leave." Her eyes glinted as she looked at Rowan.

"And what happens if I make it out?" Rowan asked.

Her mother gripped her shoulders, so tight that it hurt. "I don't know," she admitted. "I hope you'll have the power to transform back into a human again. No fairy has ever managed that before. But I believe in you, Rowan. I believe you can be the first."

Rowan caught Harold, Aiken, and Olor all looking at one another. Her mother took hold of Rowan's hand.

"Do I have to fly all the way from here?" asked Rowan.

"There are stairs cut into the rock that will take us most of the way up," said her mother. "From there it's up to you."

Rowan's head spun. She felt like someone was wrenching her insides out, but there was no time to think. The noises of the battle were getting closer. She took a deep breath and turned to Harold, Aiken, and Olor. "I'll come back. Somehow. I promise."

They all rushed forward and hugged her.

"Good luck, Oakwing," said Olor.

"Don't get eaten out there," added Aiken.

"Thank you," said Rowan. "For what you've all done."

Harold stepped forward. "No. Thank *you*, Rowan Oakwing."

Rowan felt a warmth inside that chased her fear away.

"What will you all do?" she asked, fearing for her friends' safety.

Aiken plucked an extra long stick from his belt. "We've got some unfinished business with those foxes."

She smiled and gave one last look to her friends. Then she turned and followed her mother toward the stairs.

They climbed the slippery rocks spiraling around the walls, finally reaching a stone platform high above the cavern floor. It wasn't far to the opening above from here, but it was an awfully long way down. The roar of the water pounding through the gaping mouth of the cave made it hard to think, let alone hear each other. This could be the last time that Rowan saw her mother again. The thought pricked her with the same pain that had hurt her for seven years.

"Mom," she shouted.

"You must hurry!"

"Mom, there's something I have to ask you. Before I go."

Her mother bent down to hear her over the sound of the rushing water. Rowan struggled to get the words out. It was the hardest thing for her to ask.

"They told me that the only way you can fall into this world—become a fairy—is if you think that no one cares about you."

Her mother stiffened.

"But I cared about you. So did Dad, and Willow. Didn't you know that?"

Her mother took a deep breath. "I was hurting, Rowan. I can't explain it. I never stopped loving you, your dad, or your sister. I just stopped loving . . . myself."

Rowan felt a sick feeling inside. "Was it because of me, Mom? Was it something I did?"

Rowan's mother pulled her daughter into a hug so

tight, Rowan thought she might never let go.

"Never, my love. Never. Ever."

Rowan suddenly felt lighter than she'd felt in seven years. She buried her face in her mother's robe, breathing her in one last time.

"I'm so proud of you," she heard her mother say.

The foxes were howling beneath them. Rowan wrenched herself away. She peered down to the cavern below. Vulpes wasn't there yet, but he would surely arrive any second. Harold, Aiken, Olor, and the River Fairies were bravely doing battle with the foxes and their fairy riders to stop them from getting to the foot of the staircase. Harold pecked them on the head while Aiken expertly swung his stick to fend off the orange beasts. No closing his eyes and hoping for the best anymore. Rowan smiled proudly.

"You have to go now, Rowan. Go to Dad and Willow. Carry my love to them."

"No," said a voice. It was Jack, emerging out of a darkness to hover by the rocky platform. "She's family. She belongs with us now."

Rowan's mother stepped protectively in front of her.

"It's too soon, Jack," she said hastily. "She's not in

control of her powers yet. I daren't think what Vulpes would do to her if she stayed."

"Rowan, you don't want to leave us now, do you?" said Jack. "You'd like to stay with your mother, wouldn't you? Your mother is very happy here. And you could be too."

Jack held out his hand to Rowan's mother. Her mother nervously took his hand in return.

"We know you're strong enough to stop Vulpes," said Jack. "You're the most powerful fairy anyone has ever seen!"

"I've transformed into a few . . . animals . . . but I don't think that's going to be enough to . . ."

Jack started to laugh, crouching down to get on Rowan's level.

"That's only *the beginning*! A fairy with the gift of transformation such as yours? You could control *nature herself.*"

"But I don't want to control nature. All I want is to be with my mom and dad."

The smile dropped from Jack's face.

"Okay, princess," he ordered. "Time to do your stuff. Stop playing around and sort out those foxes down there. They're making a horrible mess of my house."

"I can't—"

"Course you can! And then you can finish off Vulpes, and we can all stop hiding from him down here. I've had enough of the darkness. I want us to live in the light!"

Rowan looked to her mother, desperate for an answer.

"You *know* what you have to do," said her mother, her eyes shining with encouragement. "Wherever you are, whatever happens, you carry my love inside you. Always."

Rowan looked into her mother's eyes. Then she took a deep breath and turned to face the torrent of water above and the chasm below.

"You were wrong back then, Harold," Rowan whispered to herself. "Chicks don't get pushed off branches. *This* is how mothers teach their babies to fly."

She leapt into the void. She felt the air rushing against her face, and heard the pounding of the water above. She was determined but calm. Somehow she knew what to do this time. She could feel her muscles expanding, her neck extending, her arms spreading out into wings. And in an instant her falling had turned to flying, and her flying to soaring. She could see great white feathered wings to either side of her, and knew that she had transformed into a majestic white swan, whirling around the column of water that crashed through the space. She looked down to see Jack waving his arms madly and shouting, beseeching her to come back, but she couldn't hear him over the thunderous sound of the falling river. She took a last look below her to see her mother willing her on, and below her mother, her friends' faces turned skyward, just for a second, to see her tuck back her wings and smash through the waterfall, soaring high into the air above.

She flew higher into the night sky of Bushy Park, surrounded by a canopy of stars. Then she banked around, swooping in a large arc, fixing her mind on transformation. As she'd first done flying around Buckingham Palace, she tried to clear every other thought from her head. She whirled closer and closer to the ground, whipping through branches and skipping off the surface of the river that ran through the park. She finally hit the ground in a tumble of feathers that turned to fur. She wasn't human. She was a fox.

"I've seen what you can do. It's *very* impressive," a familiar voice slithered out in the dark night. Vulpes.

Chapter Fifteen

A HEART OF OAK

"I suppose you all thought I was down there, in that cavern, didn't you? I'm afraid I can't stand getting wet. I believe that's something we share."

Vulpes stood on the other side of the river. In the blink of an eye he leapt up, spun into fox form in midair, and landed next to her, all at such speed that one of his hands was still clenching into a furred claw as it hit the ground. Vulpes circled Rowan as she snarled at him, her lips drawing back across her fangs.

"I assume you're trying to turn back into a human?" said Vulpes. "Not as easy as you think, is it? But then, I've been trying for a lot longer than you."

Rowan scrabbled to her feet, trying once again to clear her mind, but it was impossible with Vulpes so close. Feeling defeated, her great fox limbs shrank away and she dissolved back into a fairy.

"Don't be scared," said Vulpes, still slowly wheeling around her. "You should be happy. Your mother is completely safe now. How silly I was to think she might be more powerful than me. She's nothing compared to you."

Rowan scrabbled at her throat and, with a shaking hand, held out her pendant so it pulled against her neck, knowing how important he still thought it was.

"Take it, Vulpes. Leave us all alone."

"Oh, don't worry, I *will* take it. But I'm afraid it's not that simple, is it? If I'm not the fairy of most power, it won't work for me, will it? I made that mistake last time. I should have finished off your mother while she was . . . closer. But that doesn't matter anymore. Now the only fairy more powerful than me . . . is you."

Rowan shuddered as Vulpes circled nearer.

"No more Rowan, no more problem." Vulpes was so close now, all he needed to do was whisper. "I wonder if that's what your mother was thinking when she fell into the Realms all those seven years ago? No. More. Rowan. . . ."

"No. You're wrong," said Rowan. But not with anger. Her head was clear, and she felt the strength starting to tingle through her again. "Everyone in this world felt hurt and alone once, but it's only *you* who can't seem to get over it. You don't need me. And you don't need to be human again to carry out some silly revenge. You just need to stop. Stop all of this and let everyone live in peace."

Vulpes began to shrink back into his fairy form, the hairs of his fur withdrawing back into the skin. Rowan let out a small breath of relief.

"Maybe there is some truth in what you say. Maybe not." He paused, pretending to think for a second. "But I'm having too much fun to stop now."

He sprang forward, spinning in a whirl of fur back into a snarling orange fox, bearing down on her in a fury of jaws and claws. But Rowan was too quick for him, rolling out of the way and leaping up into the air, before feeling the powerful fox muscles returning to her body. In a flash she hit the ground again as the white fox and pounced on Vulpes, her teeth snapping. She sunk her claws into his orange fur, wrestling him to the ground with more strength than she ever thought she had. They bit and scratched and rolled and growled, but before she knew it, Vulpes had pinned her to the ground beneath him. He was so close that the saliva from his jaws dripped onto her muzzle, his head pulled back, ready to land the final blow. But Rowan wasn't afraid. She was calm. She knew what to do. As Vulpes snapped forward, she shrank all her limbs and muscles at once, transforming herself into a white robin. Vulpes's jaw cracked into the ground where Rowan the fox had been seconds before, almost knocking himself out with the force of the impact. Then as he came to his senses and rolled back onto his feet, Rowan summoned all the power she could muster and transformed herself from a robin into a great white stag. She bellowed and sent the fox scurrying back to the edge of the river that poured down into the palace below. Rowan the stag stalked forward, closing in on Vulpes. The fox seemed to cringe in fear. But instead of stamping him into the ground, Rowan allowed her anger to subside. She glanced down to see her great hooves mold back into delicate fairy feet.

She may have been a tiny creature, facing down a huge fox, but Rowan no longer felt vulnerable or afraid. She felt a tingling sensation that became a growing strength that surged up from her belly and into her arms. Her senses became supersharp. It was just like that first time in St. James's Park, but on an entirely different scale. She held her arms out wide without quite knowing what she was doing. As she did so, the water in the river in front of her swelled and rose and built up into an almighty wave that loomed over Vulpes. She was commanding the very water itself. Pushing one hand forward, she sent the wave crashing over his head.

Rowan took a step forward, searching the surface of the water for any sign of Vulpes. Everything finally fell quiet, until all she could hear was the babbling of the water.

"I do so hate getting wet," came a voice from behind her.

She spun round to see the sodden fox shaking the water off behind her. In a second Vulpes was galloping toward her, jaws slavering, just like the first fox she'd met outside Hyde Park. He bore down on her, paws sending arcs of mud and spray up behind him, tongue throwing saliva into the air alongside. Only, this time she wasn't the naïve fairy that Harold had had to save. This time she knew what she had to do. Just as the fox was practically on top of her, she jumped to the side and held out her arms to summon the water up beneath her attacker. The surging river lifted Vulpes off his feet, taking him flying past Rowan toward the mouth of the waterfall. The fox howled, changing back into Vulpes's fairy form. He gave Rowan one final look of pure fury as he flew into the chasm below. Rowan ran over to the edge of the drop to peer through the cascading water down into the palace. Vulpes hit the pool in the floor of the cavern, before being swept down the underground river that led to who knew where. Beyond the river, she could see the foxes still doing battle. They caught sight of their master disappearing and took fright, racing after him down into the depths of the cave and away. Faces all turned up to Rowan, beaming with pride—Aiken, Olor, Harold, and of course, Rowan's mother.

"He's gone!" Rowan shouted down to her mother. "I'll come back to get you!" But her voice was drowned out by the sound of the raging torrent of water.

Her mom clearly couldn't hear what she was saying. Instead Rowan could see her waving a good-bye, her eyes glinting with tears.

"No! I can change back!" Rowan shouted, and she jumped and spun in the air, desperate to become a creature that could break back through the waterfall to her mother. But nothing was happening. She tried again and again, before finally crashing back to the ground.

"I'm sorry, Mom. I'm sorry. I can't do any more."

She knew that her mom couldn't hear her. She was talking more to herself now.

"Please forgive me."

As Rowan gazed down to her mother, four small words spilled from her, almost without her realizing.

"I forgive you, Mom."

Suddenly the mouth of the waterfall was shrinking, growing smaller and smaller. Or was she getting bigger?

"I forgive you," Rowan repeated quietly to herself. The gushing river was now but a stream disappearing through a big crack in the earth. She peered desperately down into the crevice but could make out no figures beneath.

"Mom!" she yelled into the darkness, scrabbling at the hole to try to make it bigger.

"We'd better shut that up," a voice said. "You never know what might fly in."

Rowan turned to see a park keeper behind her, and leapt to her feet. The park keeper wasn't much bigger than her. She wriggled her shoulder blades, but there was no sign of any wings. She was human again.

"You're up early, I'll give you that," said the park keeper. "Some kids today have trouble getting out of their bedrooms. They don't want to come to an old park full of trees and lakes. They just want the latest this and the hottest—"

"Thanks," interrupted Rowan, "but . . . I have to get back home."

"Suit yourself. Which way you headed?"

"Back into London. The smokiest bit."

"Ah, not to worry. You're always welcome back if you need to clear your head."

Rowan took a deep breath and managed a smile.

"Why don't you take the river? Lovely journey this time of the day."

"Thank you. I might just do that."

She walked back through Bushy Park in a daze, out past Hampton Court Palace toward the river. At the pier she found a riverboat captain untying his vessel. He beckoned to her to jump on.

"Welcome aboard *The Cygnus*, young lady."

Rowan gave him a puzzled look as she walked along the gangplank. She sat herself right at the front of the boat as it began steaming off back down the river, the wind whistling through her hair. She reached inside her top and pulled out her pendant. There was the small wooden oak tree with an acorn at its heart. And behind her ear she found a small, downy black feather.

A robin fluttered down and perched next to her on the handrail.

"Harold?" she asked. Some people sitting nearby stared at her, but she wasn't embarrassed. The robin cocked its head at her, then flew off downriver, toward the city. Rowan watched him leave. It couldn't have been him. She shook her head clear. She was going home.

In the playground at the bottom of Rowan's block of apartments, Jade, Jasmine, and Jessica sat on the swings, eating french fries and chicken wings as usual. A fry flew toward Rowan. Without looking she caught it and popped it into her mouth.

"Needs more ketchup," she shouted, not even breaking stride. The three girls turned to watch her as she strolled into the building, their mouths open wide. Behind her Rowan could just hear Jade cry out. She turned to see Jade gagging as she tried frantically to brush something off her tongue.

"Urgh! Something. Just. Flew. In!"

The elevator in the building was working at last, and it sped Rowan to her floor. She paused by her front door, took a deep breath, and knocked. The door cracked open, stopped against the security chain.

"Pillow!" sighed Rowan.

"Hey, Snowman, where've ya been?" said Willow. "Dad's been looking—"

But before she could finish, there was a scrabbling of the chain and the door was flung open wide. Rowan's dad burst out and lifted Rowan into a giant bear hug.

"Oh, Rowan, I thought we'd lost you, too. I'm so sorry—"

Rowan gently stopped him.

"It's all right, Dad. We're going to be all right. I promise."

He lowered her back down. Rowan leaned in close to her dad's ear to whisper.

"She's alive, Dad! And she loves you. She wanted me to tell you."

"But . . ."

"Dad. We have to find a way to bring her back. . . ."

Rowan's dad's eyes opened wide, and he turned to hold Rowan gently by the shoulders.

"Come inside, Rowan. Tell me everything."

He took each of his daughters by the hand. They stepped back into the apartment, where the morning sunshine was flooding in.

For everyone else in the block of apartments it was just a normal day. And if someone had come down the stairs at that moment, they would have seen a door closing slowly behind a father and his two daughters and imagined the same was true for them.

But it wasn't.

For them, a very special day was just beginning.

Acknowledgments

As this is my first book, there are a number of people without whose support, encouragement, and wise counsel I would never have gotten this far.

So a huge thank you goes out to David Magee, Frank Cottrell Boyce, Nick Willing, Dan MacRae, Rosie Alison, Steve Sarossy, Sue Swift, Catherine Clarke, Kirsty Robinson and Nick Hill, who all gave me the confidence that I could be the one to tell this story. Paul Webster, Peter Speyer, Simon Stephenson, Tiffany Roy and Iris, whose early reads and advice gave me the courage to share it with the world.

My incomparable agent, Claire Wilson, at Rogers, Coleridge and White, who has been the best possible confidante and guide on this journey. The fantastic Michelle Kroes at CAA.

The team at Aladdin, but especially Emma Sector, who has had such faith in a story from halfway round the world. And our cover illustrator, Jori Van Der Linde, for the beautiful picture she has painted from my words!

My mum and dad, Lynda and John Clarke, without whom I would not exist, never mind the book. Richard and Hilary Bishop, who never questioned why I was writing about fairies in their attic.

And to the first-ever reader of *Oakwing*, my wife, Rachel Clarke—for whatever kind of achievement bringing these characters to life has been, it is truly nothing next to the life that she has given to our two beautiful daughters.